Fay Weldon

was born in England and raised in New Zealand.
She took degrees in Economics and Psychology at
the University of St Andrews in Scotland and after
a decade of odd jobs and hard times began writing
fiction. She is well known as novelist, screenwriter
and cultural journalist. Her works include *The
Life and Loves of a She-Devil*, *Big Women*, *Rhode
Island Blues* and *The Bulgari Connection*, plus the
acclaimed memoir of her early life, *Auto da Fay*.

Also by Fay Weldon

Fiction

THE FAT WOMAN'S JOKE
DOWN AMONG THE
    WOMEN
FEMALE FRIENDS
REMEMBER ME
LITTLE SISTERS
PRAXIS
PUFFBALL
THE PRESIDENT'S
    CHILD
THE LIFE AND LOVES
    OF A SHE-DEVIL
THE SHRAPNEL ACADEMY
THE HEART OF
    THE COUNTRY
THE HEARTS AND
    LIVES OF MEN
THE RULES OF LIFE
LEADER OF THE BAND
THE CLONING OF JOANNA
    MAY
DARCY'S UTOPIA
GROWING RICH
LIFE FORCE
AFFLICTION
SPLITTING
WORST FEARS
BIG WOMEN
RHODE ISLAND BLUES
THE BULGARI CONNECTION

Children's Books

WOLF THE
    MECHANICAL DOG
NOBODY LIKES ME

Short Story Collections

WATCHING ME,
    WATCHING YOU
POLARIS
MOON OVER
    MINNEAPOLIS
WICKED WOMEN
A HARD TIME TO BE A
    FATHER
NOTHING TO WEAR AND
    NOWHERE TO HIDE

Non-fiction

LETTERS TO ALICE
REBECCA WEST
SACRED COWS
GODLESS IN EDEN
AUTO DA FAY

FAY WELDON

WATCHING ME, WATCHING YOU

Flamingo
An Imprint of HarperCollins*Publishers*

Flamingo
An Imprint of HarperCollins*Publishers*
77–85 Fulham Palace Road,
Hammersmith, London W6 8JB

Flamingo ® is a registered trade mark of
HarperCollins*Publishers* Ltd

www.**fire**and**water**.com

Published by Flamingo 2003
9 8 7 6 5 4 3 2 1

First published in Great Britain by
Hodder and Stoughton Ltd 1981
First published in paperback by Sceptre, an imprint of
Hodder and Stoughton Paperbacks, a division of
Hodder and Stoughton Ltd 1993

Copyright © Fay Weldon 1981

Fay Weldon asserts the moral right to be
identified as the author of this work

This collection of stories is entirely a work of fiction.
The names, characters and incidents portrayed in them are
the work of the author's imagination. Any resemblance to
actual persons, living or dead, events or localities is
entirely coincidental.

ISBN 0 00 710923 7

Typeset in Garamond 3 by Palimpsest Book Production Limited,
Polmont, Stirlingshire

Printed and bound in Great Britain by
Clays Ltd, St Ives plc

Acknowledgements

Alopecia was first published in *Winter's Tale*, Macmillan, 1976; *Angel, All Innocence* in *The Thirteenth Ghost Book*, Barrie and Jenkins, 1977; *Man with no Eyes* in *New Stories 2*, Arts Council, 1977; *Breakages* in *The Midnight Ghost Book*, Barrie and Jenkins, 1978; *Holy Stones* in *Company*, January 1979; *Spirit of the House* in *The After Midnight Ghost Book*, Hutchinson, 1980, and *Geoffrey and the Eskimo Child* in *The London Review of Books* in October 1980.

Weekend was first published in *Cosmopolitan* in October 1978 and was broadcast in the BBC radio series *Just Before Midnight*, 1979, edited by Michael Bartlett, produced by Shaun McLaughlin.

Watching Me, Watching You was a commissioned television play in the *Leap in the Dark* series, BBC Bristol, 1980, produced by Michael Croucher, directed by Colin Godman. It was first published in *Woman's Own* in January 1981.

Contents

Christmas Tree

The last thing Brian did before he came South was to plant out the Christmas Tree for his Mum and Dad. The tree had grown and flourished for years in the sooty square of Bradford backyard where all other growing things failed, except cabbages. Its needles were dark-green, thick and resilient upon the twig, and its branches grew in conventional Christmas Tree shape. Every year one or other of the Smith family would dig it out on Christmas Eve and replant it on Twelfth Night, and every year the tree repaid them by growing thicker, higher and glossier. Soot clearly suited it. So the tree had existed since 1948, when Brian was ten. Now he was twenty-five. It had given him, Brian worked out on that traumatic day, fifteen years' worth of pleasurable feelings.

'Never drops a needle on my carpet,' said his mother with pride, every year. 'Not like the ones you buy down the market.'

'They're dead before they get to you,' she would explain, every year. 'They boil the roots, you know. They don't want them growing, do they? No profit in that.'

Brian was spending a last Christmas with his Mum and Dad before leaving Bradford for good. There seemed no point in staying. His wife Audrey would not have him back, even though his daughter Helen was born that Boxing Day.

'I told you no and I meant no,' said Audrey. 'I told you if you went with that woman you needn't think you were coming back, and what I say I mean.'

Meaning what was said was a Northern habit, and in retrospect, admirable enough. At the time, however, it had seemed merely drastic. Audrey had shut him, Brian, the hero of his life, out of the cosy warmth of home; left him out in the cold exciting glitter of the unknown world, and he didn't know whether to be glad or sorry. His Mum was allowed to visit the new baby, but not his Dad. Audrey made strange distinctions. 'Pity it's not a boy,' said his Mum, cautiously. 'It's a funny-looking little thing. But Helen's a pretty name and time can work wonders.'

The affair with Carlotta had ended. Brian had written a play for the local theatre – his first. It had transferred to London. Carlotta played the lead. Brian had gone down for rehearsals. Audrey had protested. 'You'll sleep with her if you go,' she said. 'I know you. Too big for your boots.'

That was another Northern crime, being too big for your boots. Almost as bad as having a swelled head, putting on airs or having eyes bigger than your stomach. Brian slept with Carlotta, and the affair lasted for the run of the play. Four months.

'That's the way it goes,' said Alec, his agent, later to be his friend. 'When actresses say for life they mean 'til the end of the run. That's show biz.'

So Brian, who had believed he was a serious writer, and not in show biz, returned bruised and contrite to Bradford, was thrown out by Audrey, stayed with his parents over Christmas, planted out the Christmas Tree, digging the pit wide and deep, spreading the roots to maximise nourishment and minimise stress – 'That's the key to that tree's success,' said his Dad, this year as every other, 'taking care of the roots. Careful!' – and left, for London, all soft-centred harshness and painful integrity, to slam into the soft cultural underbelly of the South. And so he did.

In the year after he left Audrey Brian wrote two stage plays, one musical, four television plays for the BBC and three letters to Audrey. The applause was deafening and prolonged for everything except the letters, which were met by silence, and the silence hurt him more than the applause cheered him.

Writers tend to undervalue those who praise them, or complain that praise is patronising: whilst at the same time feeling aggrieved if they are not praised. They never win the battle with themselves, which is why, perhaps, they go on writing.

The theme of Brian's work was adoration, almost reverence, of and for the working classes, and his message a howl of hatred for the middle classes, and his solution violence.

'Wonderful!' said Alec. 'The more you insult them the more they'll love you.' And in those cosy pre-OPEC days it seemed uncomfortably true. Though that of course was not why Brian chose such themes. The theme – which was something Alec could not or would not understand – chose him. Looking around his middle-class, cheering audience, Brian suffered.

There were, of course, compensations. His words upon the page were simple and direct and attractive; and as he was upon the page, so was he in bed. The girls trailed in and out of his flat and wept when it was all, all over, and for the rest of their lives searched his work for their appearance in it, and frequently found themselves, portrayed not unsympathetically.

'I don't know how you do it,' said Alec, politely. Alec wore bifocals. He was happily married to a good cook, and a prey to romantic love for inaccessible young girls. He, at least, maintained that he was happily married. His wife had another story.

After the fourth letter, Brian forgot Audrey. He asked his parents down to London for first nights, or the taping of his Plays for Today, and they were pleased enough to stay in the grand hotels he booked them into, and his friends seemed genuinely to like them – 'What a lucky man you are, Brian, to come from a family like that. Real people!' – and if his parents went back, shaking their heads over him and his rackety life, as if he were a neighbour's child and not their own, Brian was not there to see it.
They would bring him photographs of Helen, and even a father's kind eye was obliged to observe that she was a plain and puddingy child, and that made her the easier to ignore.

He worried about himself, all the same. Had he lost his roots, forsaken his origins, worse, joined the middle classes? He had an image of himself as the Christmas Tree back home, dug up and not put back, left in its pot, unwatered, living on borrowed time, on the goodness of the past.

'Do stop *going on*,' said Victoria of the green pubic hair and feather boa. 'I never knew anyone so guilty as you. Can't you just stop worrying?'

He couldn't. Victoria left.

'But you've got it all made,' said Harriet the theatrical twin, or was it Belinda, they played the silliest games, 'rich and famous, and the revolution just around the corner, and you won't even be the first to go, like us; but the last. You good little leftie, you.'

They went, pretty soon, to be cooks on someone's charter yacht, somewhere in the sun. 'Perhaps I'm having my cake and eating it too,' he fretted to Lady Ann Scottwell, who had piano legs but wore the shortest of mini skirts, when a less secure girl would have worn trousers, and they somehow managed to make a plus out of a minus, erotically speaking. 'You might be a little naive about the revolution,' she murmured into his chest hair, cautiously. 'Daddy says it definitely isn't coming.'

That was 1968 and Daddy, it transpired, knew best.

Things went wrong. 'Violence, dear boy,' said Alec, who was going through a camp stage, 'is definitely unfashionable. There's too much of it about in real life. If things go

5

on as they are, your entire audience will be legless and armless.'

Brian, who nowadays said in public that Alec, in the great school report of life, got good marks for contracts, but bad marks for integrity, tried to take no notice. But he felt confused, as the world changed about him, and goodies became baddies – from Castro to the IRA to Israel and even cigarette smoking became unfashionable. He drank to clear the confusion.

The BBC actually rejected a script and a stage play at the Aldwych was taken off after two weeks. 'How about a film?' asked Alec. 'Hollywood calls.'

'Never,' said Brian.

'A television series? Good money. Good practice.' Brian put the phone down.

He knocked down a television producer in an Indian restaurant, appeared in Court, and was given a conditional discharge, but the *Evening Standard* picked up the story and ran a piece about Brian's recent succession of creative disasters, and referred to his 'emotional stalinism'.

'We'll sue,' said Brian to Alec.

'We won't,' said Alec to Brian. 'We'll work out what it means and see if it fits.' Alec was back on the straight and narrow path to glory.

Instead, Brian married Rea, a fragile blonde actress with a

passionate nature, who stopped him drinking by sleeping with him only when he was sober. They went back to Bradford in search of Brian's roots, but found flyovers and bypasses where the red brick back-to-backs of his childhood had been. His parents now lived on the seventeenth floor of a high-rise block. Rea did not like the place at all. Shopping baskets were filled with white sliced bread and Mr Kipling cakes, and mothers slapped their children in the streets, and youths smoked and swore on corners. 'I think you'd better forget your roots,' said Rea. She did not want anything to do with Helen, who was still not pretty, in spite of her name.

Brian and Rea set up a fashionable home and gave fashionable dinners for writers with international reputations and New York publishers and notable film directors of a non-commercial kind, mostly from Europe, and filled the house with fashionable stripped pine and Victorian biscuit tins – 'Oh the colours! Those faded reds and crimsons!' – and Brian, to give himself time to think, wrote a comedy about the upper classes and the encroaching Arabs, which did very well in the West End. 'Christ, you have sold out,' wrote Audrey, out of the blue. 'Making people laugh is a perfectly serious ambition,' he wrote back. He needed money. Rea was very expensive. He hadn't realised. She would import Batik silk just to make curtains – the yellows and browns. Ironwork had to be genuine Coalbrookdale: steak had to be fillet: clothes had to be Bonnie Cashin.

'How about doing the rewrites on a film? Rome, not Hollywood. Money's fantastic,' said Alec. 'All right,' said Brian.

Brian could not understand why, to his eye, the house

looked more and more like an old junk shop, the more Rea spent. And why she spoiled fillet steak with garlic and laughed him out of liking chips. He fell rather suddenly and startlingly out of love with Rea. She bought Christmas Trees without even the pretence of roots – merest branches posing as proper trees – and failed to deal properly with the needles, which of course would fall in profusion, so that he would find them all the year round, in piles of dust in corners and stuck, slant-wise and painful, into the fabric of his clothes. 'They've been dry-cleaned, Brian. Surely my duty to your clothes stops there?'

He felt out of sympathy with her, and rightly critical. She lived on the surface of her life: she lacked complexity. She either laughed at his moods and sensitivities, or, worse, failed to notice them. If he got drunk and hit her – which on one or two lamentable occasions happened, when he was busy rewriting the rewrites, and Rome would ring and the demand would be for this line in and this line out, taking the very last scrap of integrity from the script, and every drop of remaining dignity from himself – if he then lashed out at Rea, he had the impression that it was merely, for her, a scene in a play in which she thought she should never have accepted a part in the first place. He suffered. She would not even wear his black eye boldly, as his mother had worn his father's, but used make-up to disguise it. Everything, with Rea, was disguise, because there was no real self. She acted. She acted the part of wife, hostess, lover, connoisseur of impossible objects. She even acted being pregnant, but when it came to the point, had abortions, and then made him feel responsible by saying it was his lack of enthusiasm for the baby which induced her to have them.

8

'I didn't want to see you acting mother,' he said. 'That's true enough. At least I know what a real mother is. You don't. It's not your fault. You've had no mother.' Rea's mother had died when she was born. It was a source of some sorrow to her.

Rea had no mother, no roots, no soul. Brian felt it acutely. Times were bad between them.

Brian delivered scripts late, or sloppily written, or not at all. First drafts failed to get to second draft stage. There were arguments about broken contracts. Brian was half-pleased, half-humiliated. There seemed nothing to write about. Nothing, in a changing world, that a writer could put his finger on and cry, stop, that's it: and hold back the world for a minute or two, to allow it to look at itself.

'Tax man's at the door,' said Alec. And so he was, hammering away. 'Television series?'

'Not yet,' said Brian. 'Not quite yet.'

Brian found Rea in bed, in his and her bed, with a second-rate cameraman. 'That's it,' said Brian. 'Out!'
'Not on your nelly,' said Rea. 'You go, I'll stay.'

Rea countered, by solicitor's letter, his accusations of adultery with accusations of mental cruelty, which he could not understand, and physical cruelty, which he could. He let her have everything. 'You never were quite real to me,' he said to her, when he called to collect his clothes, in the bold New Year of 1976. 'You lived in a play.'

'You wrote it,' she said, sourly, and slammed the front door after him, and the shock made the brown Christmas Tree, stuck carelessly outside for the dustmen to collect, lose the last of its needles.

He felt the world was ending, in a sour dream. He was nearly forty, and had nothing.

'Except friends, fans, freedom, a reputation, and a queue of TV producers outside your door,' said Alec. Brian let one or two of them in. With Rea out of the way he could work properly again. He sent a large sum of money to his parents. They sent it back.

'We have everything we need,' they wrote. 'Our pensions are more than sufficient. You save it for a rainy day. You need it more than we do.'

He was hurt, feeling the reproach, and redirected the money to Audrey. She kept it, but sent no thanks.

Brian felt old. The world was full of young men in jeans, and more than a few of them were competent writers, quicker, cheaper, more sober, and harder-working than he, snatching the work from under his nose; and the best and brightest girls behaved as girls never had since the beginning of time, expecting him to make coffee and saying 'Don't ring me, I'll ring you': and the theatre had lost its shape, and its giants, and the proscenium arch had gone, and everyone ran round pretending the writer was no one special, just someone with a job to do: and a stage play had become just a television play, with a live audience.

Unsatisfactory times. The young women still came. They

preferred him, if anything, to their contemporaries. They had a surface politeness. They would ask him what the matter was, on those mornings when he turned his face to the wall, and couldn't get up, and his phone would ring, and he couldn't bring himself to answer it. 'I've lost my roots,' he'd say. They could not of course believe him, and took his mournfulness as a slur upon their sexuality, and an insult to their femininity. But what he said was at last true. He could no longer send down feelers into his past, into the black, crumbling, moving soil of his childhood.

'Re-pot yourself,' snapped Alec, who had other stars in his stable now – young men who liked, nostalgically, to dress like Colin Wilson. Alec had never stopped. 'Find new soil.'

'I tried with Rea,' said Brian.

'Now's the time to write something really big,' said Alec. 'Some spectacular statement, to hit the contemporary button on the head.'

'It's been hit so often it's lost its spring,' said Brian.

But he thought perhaps Alec was right. And he felt he was resting, not idling. He knew, as he had always known, that the big work was there somewhere, waiting to emerge: the great work, that was to be to Brian Smith and the contemporary world, as *Paradise Lost* had been to Milton and his world. The master work, the summing up, knotting up, tying up and gift presentation of the human experience that everyone was hoping for, waiting for.

11

In two acts, of course, with a small cast and a single set to minimise expense, and one good interval to maximise bar and ice-cream sales.

'Don't be like that,' said Alec. 'Playwrighting is the art of the practical.'

'One thing you have taught me, Alec,' said Brian, 'is that a writer is gigolo to the Muse, not lover.' Perhaps he should change agents? But death seemed easier.

Brian spent the Christmas of 1978 in Alec's new home, in Belgravia. One of Alec's inaccessible young girls had proved accessible, and now Alec lived with her, while Alec's wife lived with the girl's former boyfriend. 'Playing fathers and mothers,' murmured Brian into his Christmas pudding. 'Easier than husband and wife.'

But Alec's girl made a good brandy butter and her father actually worked for the Forestry Commission and the Christmas Tree in the corner had real roots, and was dark green and bouncy, and she planned to keep it in a tub out on the balcony all year, and Brian felt a real surge of affection for both of them, and a conviction that the Western World was not tottering about on its last legs, as everyone kept saying but just, as he was, having a little rest before undergoing a transfiguration into youth, health, vigour and purpose.

Almost as if this welling up of optimism attracted real reason for it, Brian fell in love in the spring of 1979.

He could not recall ever having felt such an emotion before. What he had thought was love, he now realised had been a mixture of lust and anxiety lest the object of his lust should get away, together with a soupçon of practical worry about who was to iron his shirts and wash his socks, seasoned with a pinch of pleasure at having found someone who would listen, with attention and sympathy, to the continuing soap opera of his life. In the heat and glory of his new-found love, and in the renaissance that went with it, in the new awareness of the spiritual content of what goes on, or should go on, between man and woman, he wrote to Rea, and apologised.

Rea wrote a friendly letter back, saying she was pregnant and happy and a lot of their trouble had been his, Brian's, womb-envy. Having babies, she said, was the real creativity: compared to this the writing of plays and the making of films must seem thin indeed. But the best a man could do.

He read the letter out to Linda, the object of his love. She nodded and smiled. She had long fair hair, and a pink and white complexion and tiny teeth and a little mouth, and a plump bosom and a plump figure all over. Little white hands; tiny feet. She was twenty-two. She was a country girl. Her voice, when she spoke, which she did only when entirely necessary, was faint and frail and female and had a gentle, seductive Devon burr. She was working, when he met her, as a waitress in an hotel in Weston-super-Mare, where Brian and a film crew were filming a chase sequence: a man on water skis being pursued by a beautiful CIA girl in a black wet suit.

Brian had expected, more or less, to bed the wet-suit girl sometime during their stay at the hotel: but when he saw Linda, standing against the window of the breakfast room, the morning sun shining behind her hair, silhouetting her sweet, pensive face, he lost all interest in that petty ordinary ambition. Linda brought him his orange juice, and her eyes were downcast, and he thought this is what women ought to be, and why I have had such trouble with the others: this is how my mother must have looked when she was young. Linda raised her eyes, and there was a look in them which he remembered from the Statue of the Madonna in the classroom where he'd gone for a time, when he was seven, to the Catholic school: it was of understanding, forgiveness and invitation all at once. Blue eyes beneath an alabaster brow, and the ridiculous waitress's cap narrowing the forehead, as had the Virgin Mary's wimple. He loved her.

'Christ!' said Alec. 'Are you out of your mind?'
Brian hardly thought Alec was one to talk. 'Listen,' said Alec, 'my Lisa may have been a college girl but at least she was doing English Lit and got a perfectly respectable 2–2. This girl is a waitress!'

It was only a holiday job, in actual fact. Linda's parents, he had discovered, owned a garage in East Devon and Linda lived at home, helping out.

'I'm glad she's a waitress,' said Brian. 'I'm finally back where I belong. Amongst real people, who do real things, and live simple, honest hard-working lives.'

'Christ!' was all Alec would say.

During that long hot summer Brian wrote a four-part love story for television so full of sensual delights that even enemies and critics were touched, and Alec was silent, and Audrey wrote, out of the blue. 'My God,' said Audrey, 'life was never like that for you and me. Wish it had been. My fault, perhaps. Helen's training as a nurse. Shouldn't you be using your television time to protest about low pay instead of all this full-frontal stuff?'

Still, it was better than nothing.

Linda came to live with him in London. She wouldn't and didn't sleep with him, though nobody believed it. She was virtuous. Her family didn't believe it either and cast her off. She spent her time writing letters home on thin blue lined paper with purple violets round the edge. She had unformed, careful writing and her spelling was bad. He found that charming. He still had trouble spelling, himself.

Forgiveness was a long time coming.

'I've let them down,' she whispered. 'They trusted me.'

'Perhaps we ought to be married,' said Brian, though he'd sworn publicly never to do anything like that again. She considered.

'I suppose that would be nice,' said Linda. 'They'd forgive me, then. Oh, I do so want you to meet them! I miss my mother and my brothers so much.'

They agreed to marry at Christmas. It couldn't be any earlier because Brian had to go to Los Angeles for three months, to work on a film. A thriller.

He half-wondered whether to take Linda, but she said firmly that she didn't want to come. 'I'll stay home and arrange the wedding,' she said. 'Honestly, I'd rather. I don't really fit in with your smart friends.'

'That's what's so wonderful about you,' he said. He could see that in Los Angeles, where girls were thin and leggy and bronzed, she might not appear to advantage. She liked to keep out of the sun, because it made her nose peel.

He had thought the wedding would be a Register Office affair, but Linda had set her heart on being married in a white dress with bell sleeves in the village church, and he agreed. 'It will cost you to do it properly,' she said, timorously. She had never asked for money before. He gave her a cheque. 'I haven't got a bank account,' she said.
'If you're going home,' he said, 'your parents can cash it for you.'
'They don't have banks,' she said, and he was surprised. What kind of people were they? 'It's only a little garage,' she apologised.

He was pleased. He thought the peasant soil might be some kind of equivalent to the proletarian earth that afforded his early nourishment. He flew off to LA over the Pole, first class, and did not even try to date the young woman who sat next to him, who wore sneakers and had a little silver snuff box full of vitamin pills and said she was in hospitals. 'Administration?' he asked.

'I own them,' she said, and what with East turning West beneath them, and the sun rising where it had only just set, and rather too much champagne, he felt the world was upside-down and longed for Linda's stolid charm, and her little feet in high strap heels, rather than those serviceable if sexy sneakers. Stolid? He was rather shocked by that particular choice of word. It was not how one usually described the Virgin Mary. Stolid.

In love with the Virgin Mary. But he was. He became almost nauseous when confronted with the ravishing Mary Magdalenas of Malibu Beach: human animals doing their copulatory dance under the Studio Ring Master's whip: the fantasies of an exhausted film industry, taken such definite flesh. He had no trouble resisting them.

It was not, he saw now, that he had ever been promiscuous. Just that no woman until now had ever succeeded in properly captivating him. 'Christ!' said Alec on the telephone, across half the world. But he'd put his commission up to fifteen per cent and since the spring, and the advent of Linda, Brian had been doing well enough and fulfilling his early promise, as money maker if not saviour of society.

Brian came home on December 14. The wedding was on December 15. Linda was already in Devon. The wedding was all organised, she told him when he rang from Heathrow. All that was required was Brian's appearance, wearing a suit, and with the ring, early the next morning. She'd even arranged the cars, which should have been the groom's task. The wedding reception was to be in the Women's Institute Hall, and they were to spend the night with Linda's parents, the Joneses, in the caravan in the garden. If it was raining, or snowing, they could squeeze into her bedroom.

Women's Institute? Caravan? In December? After Studio City, Malibu and Sunset Boulevard, it sounded strange.

17

But Brian Smith marrying Linda Jones sounded profoundly, agreeably right.

He was relieved, too, if only by virtue of shortage of time, of the burden of providing friends and family to witness the wedding. He wanted a new life. He did not want the past clouding any issues. In East Devon, down in the South West, he would be born again.

Honest rural folk.

Linda's father met him at the station. The train was late. Mr Jones paced up and down in an ill-fitting navy suit, and boots with buckled uppers. No more ill-fitting, Brian told himself, than my father's at prize day at the grammar school. The pale grey suits of the executives of Studio City, their smooth after-shaved jowls, their figures jogged into shape, made an unfair comparison. Linda's father was narrow like a ferret, sharp-eyed like a fox, untidy as an unpruned hedge in autumn, and had thick red hands with bleak oil beneath the nails. One eye wandered, when he spoke.

'Best hurry,' said Mr Jones, 'Linda's waiting,' and they climbed into an old C-registration Mini, with the back seats taken out and piled with plastic fertiliser sacks and ropes, guarded by a snappy, noisy, ugly little dog. Barking prevented them from talking.

The garage had a single petrol pump, and was marked No Petrol, and was outside the last house in an undistinguished row of pre-war houses set back from the main road. Brian was rushed upstairs to change, the dog snapping at his heels, into a tiny room with four different flowered papers on the wall, and two beds and three wardrobes and six trays of sausage rolls on boards placed across the beds. He caught a glimpse of Linda as he fled from the dog; she was in brilliant Terylene white. He thought she blew him a kiss.

What am I doing, he thought, trying to find a place between the plastic beads and greeting cards and Mr Men stickers and the Christmas holly and bells which decked the mirror, so he could fix his tie. He was bronzed by the Californian sun; his face was narrow and handsome and clever. What am I doing? What desperation has landed me here? No, this is jet-lag speaking. I love Linda. Write it in plastic Christmas foam on what remains of the mirror. I love Linda. What has Linda's family to do with her, any more than mine to do with me? Roots. Aye, there's the rub. Red Devon soil hardened by winter. What good was that to him? He was used to soot. He was ready. A Rolls-Royce stood outside. Well, he was paying.

Into the first car he stepped, and Linda's father came with him. Best man. Linda's father had trodden in the mess left by the dog in the hall. Linda's father's shoe smelt. 'Overexcited,' said Linda's mother. She was stout and dressed in green satin but otherwise might have been anyone. Linda's cross-eyed brother kicked the dog out of the house. Linda's wall-eyed brother hoovered up the mess, which was largely liquid.

'Don't do that!' cried Linda's mother. Linda smiled serenely beneath her white white veil. She was a virgin.

'My wedding day is the happiest day of my life,' she said, though whether to Brian as he passed, or as a statement of policy to God above, or simply to quell the riot he did not know. Mr Jones nipped upstairs to clean his shoe.

The village church was big and handsome and very cold. A hundred people or so were gathered on the Bride's side of the church. The acoustics were bad, and there were many small children in the congregation. Brian stood dazed, facing the cross and banks of paper flowers. The Vicar was elderly and dressed in a white gown. Brian heard sound and movement and presently Linda stood beside him, and he felt better, and to the sound of children crying and protesting he and she were married, in God's sight.

Outside the church, later, there were many photographs taken. He thought he had never seen so many ugly and misshapen people gathered together in one place. He could not be sure whether this was so, and a phenomenon peculiar to this part of Devon, or whether it was just the sudden contrast to the people of Southern California.

Various people young and old, men and women, came up to congratulate him, and in the course of brief conversations let it be known that Linda was not a virgin, had had at least two relationships with married men, one abortion, one miscarriage and had married him for his money. Linda did not seem to be popular. He thought perhaps he was dreaming.

At the reception at the W I Hall, where sherry was served, and also the sausage rolls he had seen on the bed, the Vicar remarked on the cross- and wall-eyes of the Jones boys, and accounted for it by village in-breeding. It's a genetic weakness, he said. Genetics, he added, bitterly, was

20

a three-syllable word, and words so long were not often heard in these parts.

Jet lag became more pressing. He had to sleep. He remembered making a speech. Linda put on her going-away clothes and the Rolls took them back to the garage. The dog lay vomiting on the path.

'Now we can,' said Linda, 'quick! Before anyone comes home,' and she pulled him upstairs to the room with the many wallpapers and he removed her clothes except her veil and made love to her. That was what marriage was all about. He thought she probably wasn't a virgin, but just pretending. He wondered where his silver cuff links were and couldn't see them. Then he fell asleep. When he woke she was unpacking wedding presents, and singing happily. 'This is the happiest day of my life! Oh, how I love you!' said Linda, and gave him a kiss. 'Look, a toaster, and a lovely casserole with yellow flowers. That's from Auntie Ann.'

She had not noticed any lack of sexual enthusiasm in him. Was that innocence, or insensitivity, or cunning? His cuff links were decidedly gone. 'You must have left them in London,' said Linda. 'They'll turn up.'

They had been a present from Rea. For some reason he valued them. But Linda dismissed the matter. Now they were married she seemed much more definite. Her eyelids no longer drooped, in modesty and decorum. She looked him straight in the eye, and lied.

'The bill from the caterers hasn't been paid. Could you possibly give me a cheque? Three hundred pounds.'

21

'I thought you made the food yourselves.'

'No. It was all bought in. Every scrap.' She did not seem to mind that the lie was easily detected, nor the amount improbable. She gave him a little kiss on the nose. 'Husband! Go on, say wife.'

'Wife!'

'Will you come out with us on the Christmas Trees? It would please Dad.'

And so they did. Dad and the two boys and Brian, after dark on his wedding night, with light snow falling, took shovels and borrowed a neighbour's van and travelled ten miles inland, on to Forestry Commission land, where the pylons were slung from hill to hill, carrying electricity from the Nuclear Power Station to the good folk of Exeter, and there, beneath the wires, hair crackling and tooth fillings zinging, they pirated Christmas Trees. Good healthy well-shaped trees, three foot high, with a broad spread of vigorous roots. Brian dug, and laughed, and dug some more. It was theft, it was dangerous, there were dog patrols to stop such acts, but he felt, at last, that he was doing something sensible and useful. The Jones family were pleased by the muscle and enthusiasm of their new relative. Father Jones, despite the snow, took off his coat, and carefully laid it down beside where Brian rested, and on impulse Brian felt in the inside pocket, and yes, there were his silver cuff links. He left them where they were, and said nothing. What was there to say?

He didn't suppose the dog was trained to cause uproar: no

one was clever enough for that: just that when the dog
caused uproar, the cover seemed too good to miss. He
thought Mrs Jones might well feed it on cascara, just to
be on the safe side.

The hilarity of exhaustion and despair turned sour when
they arrived back at the house with some fifty Christmas
Trees and unloaded them in the backyard. Mrs Jones had an
old tin bath ready outside the back door, filled with boiling
water. The brother with the wall-eyes bound the living green
of the trees with twine. Mrs Jones dumped the roots in the
boiling water, and the cross-eyed brother reloaded them on
to the van. Linda stood by and watched the murder. 'What
are you doing? Why?' he shouted at them, but the wind
was strong, and snow flicked off the ground, and the water
bubbled, and the stereo in the house was on loud to cover
their nefarious deed. Cliff Richard. He thought he could
hear the trees screaming as they died. 'Just boiling them,'
said Linda, surprised.
'But why, why?'
'It's just what we do.'
'It can't make any difference to you,' he cried. 'No profit
lost to you if they grow.'
'People always boil the roots,' she said, looking at him as if
he was daft. 'It's the done thing.'

He could see she took him for a fool, and despised him for it,
and had tricked him and trapped him, for all he was bright
and old, and she was thick and young.

He stumbled inside and up to the bedroom and fell asleep
and slept, with the smell of boiling tree in his nostrils,
and flakes of sausage-roll pastry in the sheets, and woke,

with Linda next to him. Her skin was clammy. She wore a cerise nylon nightie, trimmed with fawn nylon lace. He went downstairs to the coin telephone in the hall and rang Alec. 'I think I've found the right place for me,' he said, and indeed he had. He had bound himself by accident to a monstrous family in a monstrous place and had discovered by accident what he felt to be the truth, long evident, long evaded. It was that human nature was irredeemable.

'I think I'll stay down here for a while with my wife,' he said. My wife! All aspirations and ambition had been burned away: old wounds cauterised with so sudden and horrific a knife as to leave him properly cleansed, and purified.

'Next to nature,' said Brian with a dreadful animation rising in him: the writer's animation; 'with cows and cider and power lines and kind and honest country folk. I think I could really write down here!'

'Christ!' said Alec. He seemed to have fewer and fewer words to rub together, as his stable of writers found more and more.

Breakages

'We blossom and flourish
As leaves on a tree,
And wither and perish
But nought changeth thee —'

sang David's congregation in its laggardly, quavery voice. Some trick of acoustics made much of what happened in the church audible in the vicarage kitchen, where tonight, as so often, Deidre sat and darned socks and waited for Evensong to end.

The vicarage, added as a late Victorian afterthought, leaned up against the solidity of the Norman church. The house was large, ramshackle, dark and draughty, and prey to wet rot, dry rot, woodworm and beetle. Here David and Deidre lived. He was a vicar of the established Church; she was his wife. He attended to the spiritual welfare of his parishioners: she presided over the Mothers' Union and the Women's Institute and ran the Amateur Dramatic Society. They had been married for twenty-one years. They had no children, which was a source of acute disappointment to them and to Deidre's mother, and of understandable disappointment to the parish. It is always pleasant, in a small, stable and increasingly elderly community, to watch other people's children grow up, and sad to be deprived of that pleasure.

25

'Oh no, please,' said Deidre, now, to the Coronation Mug on the dresser. It was a rare piece, produced in anticipation of an event which had never occurred: the Coronation of the Duke of Windsor. The mug was, so far, uncracked and unchipped, and worth some three hundred pounds, but had just moved to the very edge of its shelf, not smoothly and purposively, but with an uneven rocking motion which made Deidre hope that entreaty might yet calm it, and save it from itself. And indeed, after she spoke, the mug was quiet, and lapsed into the ordinary stillness she had once always associated with inanimate objects.

> *'Immortal, invisible,*
> *God only wise –*
> *In light inaccessible –'*

Deidre joined in the hymn, singing gently and soothingly, and trying to feel happy, for the happier she felt the fewer the breakages there would be and perhaps one day they would stop altogether, and David would never, ever find out that one by one, the ornaments and possessions he most loved and valued were leaping off shelves and shattering, to be secretly mended by Deidre with such skills as she remembered from the early days, before marriage had interrupted her training in china restoration, and her possible future in the Victoria and Albert Museum.

Long ago and far away. Now Deidre darned. David's feet were sensitive to anything other than pure, fine wool. Not for him the tough nylon mixtures that other men wore. Deidre darned.

The Coronation Mug rocked violently.

'Stop it,' said Deidre, warningly. Sometimes to appear stern was more effective than to entreat. The mug stayed where it was. But just a fraction further and it would have fallen.

Deidre unpicked the last few stitches. She was in danger of cobbling the darn, and there is nothing more uncomfortable to sensitive skin than a cobbled darn.

'You do it on purpose,' David would complain, not without reason. Deidre's faults were the ones he found most difficult to bear. She was careless, lost socks, left lids unscrewed, taps running, doors open, saucepans burning: she bought fresh bread when yesterday's at half price would do. It was her nature, she maintained, and grieved bitterly when her husband implied that it was wilful and that she was doing it to annoy. She loved him, or said so. And he loved her, or said so.

The Coronation Mug leapt off its shelf, arced through the air and fell and broke in two pieces at Deidre's feet. She put the pieces at the very back of the drawer beneath the sink. There was no time for mending now. Tomorrow morning would have to do, when David was out parish-visiting, in houses freshly dusted and brightened for his arrival. Fortunately, David seldom inspected Deidre's drawer. It smelt, when opened, of dry rot, and reminded him forcibly of the large sums of money which ought to be spent on the repair of the house, and which he did not have.

'We could always sell something,' Deidre would sometimes venture, but not often, for the suggestion upset him. David's mother had died when he was four; his father had gone bankrupt when he was eight; relatives had reared him and

27

sent him off to boarding school where he had been sexually and emotionally abused. Possessions were his security.

She understood him, forgave him, loved him and tried not to argue.

She darned his socks. It was, today, a larger pile than usual. Socks kept disappearing, not by the pair, but singly. David had lately discovered a pillowslip stuffed full of them pushed to the back of the wardrobe. It was his wife's deceit which worried him most, or so he said. Hiding socks! That and the sheer careless waste of it all. Losing socks! So Deidre tried tying the socks together for the wash, and thus, in pairs, the night before, spun and dried, they had lain in the laundry basket. In the morning she had found them in one ugly, monstrous knot, and each sock oddly long, as if stretched by a hand too angry to know what it was doing. Rinsing had restored them, fortunately, to a proper shape, but she was obliged to darn where the stretching had worn the fabric thin.

It was always like this: always difficult, always upsetting. David's things were attacked, as if the monstrous hand were on her side, yet it was she, Deidre, who had to repair the damage, follow its source as it moved about the house, mending what it broke, wiping tomato purée from the ceiling, toothpaste from the lavatory bowl, replanting David's seedlings, rescrewing lids, closing doors, refolding linen, turning off taps. She scarcely dared leave the house for fear of what might happen in her absence, and this David interpreted as lack of interest in his parish. Disloyalty, to God and husband.

And so it was, in a way. Yet they loved each other. Man and wife.

Deidre's finger was bleeding. She must have cut it on the sharp edge of the broken Coronation Mug. She opened the table drawer and took out the first piece of cloth which came to hand, and wrapped her finger. The cold tap started to run of its own accord, but she ignored it. Blood spread out over the cloth but presently, fortunately, stopped.

Could you die from loss of blood, from a small finger cut?

The invisible hand swept the dresser shelf, knocking all sorts of treasures sideways but breaking nothing. It had never touched the dresser before, as if awed, as Deidre was, by the ever increasing value of its contents – rare blue and white pieces, frog mugs, barbers' bowls, lustre cups, a debatably Ming bowl, which a valuer said might well fetch five thousand pounds.

Enough to paint the vicarage, inside, and install central heating, and replaster walls and buy a new vacuum cleaner.

The dresser rattled and shook: she could have sworn it slid towards her.

David did not give Deidre a housekeeping allowance. She asked for money when she needed it, but David seldom recognised that it was in fact needed. He could not see the necessity of things like washing-up liquid, sugar, toilet rolls, new scourers. Sometimes she stole money from his pocket:

once she took a coin out of the offertory on Sunday morning instead of putting a coin in it.

Why did she stoop to it? She loved him.

A bad wife, a barren wife, and a poor sort of person.

David came home. The house fell quiet, as always, at his approach. Taps stopped running and china rattling. David kissed her on her forehead.

'Deidre,' said David, 'what have you wrapped around your finger?'

Deidre, curious herself, unwrapped the binding and found that she had used a fine lace and cotton handkerchief, put in the drawer for mending, which once had belonged to David's grandmother. It was now sodden and bright, bright red.

'I cut my finger,' said Deidre, inadequately and indeed foolishly, for what if he demanded to know what had caused the wound? But David was too busy rinsing and squeezing the handkerchief under the tap to enquire. Deidre put her finger in her mouth and put up with the salt, exciting taste of her own blood.

'It's hopelessly stained,' he mourned. 'Couldn't you just for once have used something you wouldn't spoil? A tissue?'

David did not allow the purchase of tissues. There had been none in his youth: why should they be needed now, in his middle age?

'I'm sorry,' said Deidre, and thought, as she spoke, 'I am always saying sorry, and always providing cause for my own remorse.'

He took the handkerchief upstairs to the bathroom, in search of soap and a nailbrush. 'What kind of wife are you, Deidre?' he asked as he went, desperate.

What kind, indeed? Married in a register office in the days before David had taken to Holy Orders and a Heavenly Father more reliable than his earthly one. Deidre had suggested that they remarry in church, as could be and had been done by others, but David did not want to. Hardly a wife at all.

A barren wife. A fig tree, struck by God's ill temper. David's God. In the beginning they had shared a God, who was bleak, plain, sensible and kind. But now, increasingly, David had his own jealous and punitive God, whom he wooed with ritual and richness, incense and images, dragging a surprised congregation with him. He changed his vestments three times during services, rang little bells to announce the presence of the Lord, swept up and down aisles, and in general seemed not averse to being mistaken for God.

The water pipes shrieked and groaned as David turned on the tap in the bathroom, but that was due to bad plumbing rather than unnatural causes. She surely could not be held responsible for that, as well.

When the phenomena – as she thought of them – first started, or rather leapt from the scale of ordinary domestic

31

carelessness to something less explicable and more sinister, she went to the doctor.

'Doctor,' she said, 'do mumps in adolescence make men infertile?'
'It depends,' he said, proving nothing. 'If the gonads are affected it well might. Why?'

No reason had been found for Deidre's infertility. It lay, presumably, like so much else, in her mind. She had had her tubes blown, painfully and unforgettably, to facilitate conception, but it had made no difference. For fifteen years twenty-three days of hope had been followed by five days of disappointment, and on her shoulders rested the weight of David's sorrow, as she, his wife, deprived him of his earthly immortality, his children.

'Of course,' he said sadly, 'you are an only child. Only children are often infertile. The sins of the fathers –' David regarded fecundity as a blessing; the sign of a woman in tune with God's universe. He had married Deidre, he vaguely let it be known, on the rebound from a young woman who had gone on to have seven children. Seven!

David's fertility remained unquestioned and unexamined. A sperm count would surely have proved nothing. His sperm was plentiful and he had no sexual problems that he was aware of. To ejaculate into a test-tube to prove a point smacked uncomfortably of onanism.

The matter of the mumps came up during the time of Deidre's menopause, a month or so after her, presumably, last period. David had been in the school sanatorium with mumps: she had heard him saying so to a distraught mother, adding, 'Oh mumps! Nothing in a boy under fourteen. Be thankful he has them now, not later.'

So he was aware that mumps were dangerous, and could render a man infertile. And Deidre knew well enough that David had lived in the world of school sanatoria after the age of fourteen, not before. Why had he never mentioned mumps? And while she wondered, and pondered, and hesitated to ask, toothpaste began to ooze from tubes, and rose trees were uprooted in the garden, and his seedlings trampled by unseen boots, and his clothes in the wardrobe tumbled in a pile to the ground, and Deidre stole money to buy mending glue, and finally went to the doctor.

'Most men,' said the doctor, 'confuse impotence with infertility and believe that mumps cause the former, not the latter.'

Back to square one. Perhaps he didn't know.

'Why have you *really* come?' asked the doctor, recently back from a course in patient–doctor relations. Deidre offered him an account of her domestic phenomena, as she had not meant to do. He prescribed Valium and asked her to come back in a week. She did.

'Any better? Does the Valium help?'
'At least when I see things falling, I don't mind so much.'
'But you still see them falling?'
'Yes.'
'Does your husband see them too?'

33

'He's never there when they do.'

Now what was any thinking doctor to make of that?

'We could try hormone replacement therapy,' he said.
'No,' said Deidre. 'I am what I am.'
'Then what do you want me to do?'

'If I could only feel angry with my husband,' said Deidre,
'instead of forever understanding and forgiving him, I might
get it to stop. As it is, I am releasing too much kinetic
energy.'

There were patients waiting. They had migraines, eczema
and boils. He gave her more Valium, which she did not
take.

Deidre, or some expression of Deidre, went home and
churned up the lawn and tore the gate off its hinges. The
other Deidre raked and smoothed, resuscitated and blamed a
perfectly innocent child for the gate. A child. It would have
taken a forty-stone giant to twist the hinges so, but no one
stopped, fortunately, to think about that. The child went
to bed without supper for swinging on the vicar's gate.

The wound on Deidre's finger gaped open in an unpleasant
way. She thought she could see the white bone within the
bloodless flesh.

Deidre went upstairs to the bathroom, where David washed
his wife's blood from his grandmother's hankie. 'David,' said
Deidre, 'perhaps I should have a stitch in my finger?'

David had the toothmug in his hand. His jaw was open, his eyes wide with shock. He had somehow smeared toothpaste on his black lapel. 'The toothmug has recently been broken, and very badly mended. No one told me. Did you do it?'

The toothmug dated from the late eighteenth century and was worn, cracked and chipped, but David loved it. It had been one of the first things to go, and Deidre had not mended it with her usual care, thinking, mistakenly, that one more crack amongst so many would scarcely be noticed.

'I am horrified,' said David.
'Sorry,' said Deidre.
'You always break my things, never your own.'
'I thought that when you got married,' said Deidre, with the carelessness of desperation, for surely now David would start an inspection of his belongings and all would be discovered, 'things stopped being yours and mine, and became ours.'
'Married! You and I have never been married, not in the sight of God, and I thank Him for it.'

There. He had said what had been unsaid for years, but there was no relief in it, for either of them. There came a crash of breaking china from downstairs. David ran down to the kitchen, where the noise came from, but could see no sign of damage.

He moved into the living room. Deidre followed, dutifully.

'You've shattered my life,' said David. 'We have nothing in common. You have been a burden since the beginning. I wanted a happy, warm, loving house. I wanted children.'

'I suppose,' said Deidre, 'you'll be saying next that my not having children is God's punishment?'

'Yes,' said David.

'Nothing to do with your mumps?'

David was silent, taken aback. Out of the corner of her eye Deidre saw the Ming vase move. 'You're a sadistic person,' said David eventually. 'Even the pains and humiliations of long ago aren't safe from you. You revive them.'

'You knew all the time,' said Deidre. 'You were infertile, not me. You made me take the blame. And it's too late for me now.'

The Ming vase rocked to the edge of the shelf: Deidre moved to push it back, but not quickly enough. It fell and broke.

David cried out in pain and rage. 'You did it on purpose,' he wept. 'You hate me.'

Deidre went upstairs and packed her clothes. She would stay with her mother while she planned some kind of new life for herself. She would be happier anywhere in the world but here, sharing a house with a ghost.

David moved through the house, weeping, but for his treasures, not for his wife. He took a wicker basket and in it laid tenderly – as if they were the bodies of children – the many broken and mended vases and bowls and dishes which he found. Sometimes the joins were skilful and barely detectable to his moving forefinger: sometimes careless. But everything was spoilt. What had been perfect was now second-rate and without value. The finds in the junk shops, the gifts from old ladies, the few small knick-knacks which had come to him from his dead mother – his whole past destroyed by his wife's single-minded malice and cunning.

He carried the basket to the kitchen, and sat with his head in his hands.

Deidre left without saying another word. Out of the door, through the broken garden gate, into the night, through the churchyard, for the powers of the dead disturbed her less than the powers of the living, and to the bus station.

David sat. The smell of rot from the sink drawer was powerful enough, presently, to make him lift his head.

The cold tap started to run. A faulty washer, he concluded. He moved to turn it off, but the valve was already closed. 'Deidre!' he called, 'what have you done with the kitchen tap?' He did not know why he spoke, for Deidre had gone.

The whole top of the dresser fell forward to the ground. Porcelain shattered and earthenware powdered. He could hear the little pings of the Eucharist bell in the church next door, announcing the presence of God.

He thought perhaps there was an earthquake, but the central light hung still and quiet. Upstairs heavy feet bumped to and fro, dragging, wrenching and banging. Outside the window the black trees rocked so fiercely that he thought he would be safer in than out. The gas taps of the cooker were on and he could smell gas, mixed with fumes from the coal fire where Deidre's darning had been piled up and was now smouldering. He closed his eyes.

He was not frightened. He knew that he saw and heard these things, but that they had no substance in the real world. They were a distortion of the facts, as water becomes wine in the Communion service, and bread becomes the flesh of the Saviour.

When next he opened his eyes the dresser was restored, the socks still lay in the mending basket, the air was quiet.

Sensory delusions, that was all, brought about by shock. But unpleasant, all the same. Deidre's fault. David went upstairs to sleep but could not open the bedroom door. He thought perhaps Deidre had locked it behind her, out of spite. He was tired. He slept in the spare room, peacefully, without the irritant of Deidre's warmth beside him.

In the morning, however, he missed her, and as if in reply to his unspoken request she reappeared, in the kitchen, in time to make his breakfast tea. 'I spent the night in the hospital,' she said. 'I went to casualty to have a stitch put in my finger, and I fainted, and they kept me in.'

Her arm was in a sling.

'I'm sorry,' he said. 'You should have told me it was a bad cut and I'd have been more sympathetic. Where did you put the bedroom key?'

'I haven't got it,' she said, and the teapot fell off the table and there were tea and tea leaves everywhere, and, one-armed, she bungled the business of wiping it up. He helped.

'You shouldn't put breakables and spillables on the edge of tables,' he reproached her. 'Then it wouldn't happen.'

'I suppose not.'

'I'm sorry about what I may have said last night. Mumps are a sore point. I thought I would die from the itching, and my friends just laughed.'

Itching? Mumps?

'Mumps *is* the one where you come out in red spots and they tie your hands to stop you scratching?'

'No. That's chickenpox,' she said.

'Whatever it was, if you're over fourteen you get it very badly indeed and it is humiliating to have your hands tied.'

'I can imagine.'

He wrung out the dishcloth. The tap, she noticed, was not dripping. 'I'm sorry about your things,' she said. 'I should have told you.'

'Am I such a frightening person?'

'Yes.'

'They're only things,' he said, to her astonishment. The house seemed to take a shift back into its ordinary perspective. She thought, that though childless, she could still live an interesting and useful life. Her friends with grown-up children, gone away, complained that it was as if their young had never been. The experience of childrearing was that, just that, no more, no less. An experience without much significance, presently over; as lately she had experienced the behaviour of the material world.

David insisted that Deidre must surely have the bedroom key, and was annoyed when she failed to produce it. 'Why would I lock you out of the bedroom?' she asked.

39

'Why would you do anything!' he remarked dourly. His gratitude for her return was fading: his usual irritation with her was reasserting itself. She was grateful for familiar ways, and as usual animated by them.

He went up the ladder to the bedroom window, and was outraged. 'I've never seen a room in such a mess,' he reported, from the top of the ladder, a figure in clerical black perched there like some white-ruffled crow. 'How you did all that, even in a bad temper, I can't imagine!'

The heavy wardrobe was on its side, wedged against the door: the bed was upside down: the chairs and light bulb broken, and the bedclothes, tumbled and knotted, had the same stretched and strained appearance as David's socks; and the carpet had been wrenched up, tossing furniture as it lifted, and wrung out like a dishcloth.

When the wardrobe had been moved back into place, the door was indeed found to be locked, with the key on the inside of the door, but both preferred not to notice that.

'I'm sorry,' said Deidre, 'I was upset about our having no children. That, and my time of life.'
'All our times of life,' he said. 'And as to your having no children, if it's anyone's fault, it's God's.'

Together they eased the carpet out of the window and down onto the lawn, and patiently and peaceably unwrung it. But the marks of the wringing stayed, straying for ever across the bedroom floor, to remind them of the dangers of, for him, petulance, and for her, the tendency to blame others for her own shortcomings.

40

Presently the Ming vase was mended, not by Deidre but by experts. He sold it and they installed central heating and had a wall knocked out there, a window put in here, and the washer on the kitchen tap mended, and the dry rot removed so that the sink drawer smelled like any other, and the broken floorboard beneath the dresser replaced. The acoustics in the kitchen changed, so that Deidre could no longer hear David's services as she sat by the fire, so she attended church rather more often; and David, she soon noticed, dressed up as God rather less, and diverted his congregation's attention away from himself and more towards the altar.

Alopecia

It's 1972.

'Fiddlesticks,' says Maureen. Everyone else says 'crap' or 'balls', but Maureen's current gear, being Victorian sprigged muslin, demands an appropriate vocabulary. 'Fiddlesticks. If Erica says her bald patches are anything to do with Derek, she's lying. It's alopecia.'

'I wonder which would be worse,' murmurs Ruthie in her soft voice, 'to have a husband who tears your hair out in the night, or to have alopecia.'

Ruthie wears a black fringed satin dress exactly half a century old, through which, alas, Ruthie's ribs show even more prominently than her breasts. Ruthie's little girl Poppy (at four too old for playgroup, too young for school), wears a long, white (well, yellowish) cotton shift which contrasts nicely with her mother's dusty black.

'At least the husband might improve, with effort,' says Alison, 'unlike alopecia. You wake up one morning with a single bald patch and a month or so later there you are, completely bald. Nothing anyone can do about it.' Alison, plump mother of three, sensibly wears a flowered Laura Ashley dress which hides her bulges.

'It might be quite interesting,' remarks Maureen. 'The egghead approach. One would have to forgo the past, of course, and go all space age, which would hardly be in keeping with the mood of the times.'

'You are the mood of the times, Maureen,' murmurs Ruthie, as expected. Ruthie's simple adulation of Maureen is both gratifying and embarrassing, everyone agrees.

Everyone agrees, on the other hand, that Erica Bisham of the bald patches is a stupid, if ladylike, bitch.

Maureen, Ruthie and Alison are working in Maureen's premises off the Kings Road. Here Maureen, as befits the glamour of her station, the initiator of Mauromania, meets the media, expresses opinions, answers the phone, dictates to secretaries (male), selects and matches fabrics, approves designs and makes, in general, multitudinous decisions – although not, perhaps, as multitudinous as the ones she was accustomed to make in the middle and late sixties, when the world was young and rich and wild. Maureen is forty but you'd never think it. She wears a large hat by day (and, one imagines, night) which shades her anxious face and guards her still pretty complexion. Maureen leads a rich life. Maureen once had her pubic hair dyed green to match her fingernails – or so her husband Kim announced to a waiting (well, such were the days) world: she divorced him not long after, having lost his baby at five months. The head of the foetus, rumour had it, emerged green, and her National Health Service GP refused to treat her any more,

43

and she had to go private after all – she with her Marxist convictions.

That was 1968. If the State's going to tumble, let it tumble. The sooner the better. Drop out, everyone! Mauromania magnifique! And off goes Maureen's husband Kim with Maureen's au pair – a broad-hipped, big-bosomed girl, good breeding material, with an ordinary coarse and curly brush, if somewhat reddish.

Still, it had been a good marriage as marriages go. And as marriages go, it went. Or so Maureen remarked to the press, on her way home (six beds, six baths, four recep., American kitchen, patio, South Ken) from the divorce courts. Maureen cried a little in the taxi, when she'd left her public well behind, partly from shock and grief, mostly from confusion that beloved Kim, Kim, who so despised the nuclear family, who had so often said that he and she ought to get divorced in order to have a true and unfettered relationship, that Maureen's Kim should have speeded up Maureen's divorce in order to marry Maureen's au pair girl before the baby arrived. Kim and Maureen had been married for fifteen years. Kim had been Kevin from Liverpool before seeing the light or at any rate the guru. Maureen had always been just Maureen from Hoxton, East London: remained so through the birth, rise and triumph of Mauromania. It was her charm. Local girl makes good.

Maureen has experience of life: she knows by now, having also been married to a psychiatrist who ran off with all her money and the marital home, that it is wise to watch what people do, not listen to what they say. Well, it's something to have learned. Ruthie and Alison, her (nominal) partners from the beginning, each her junior by some ten years, listen to Maureen with respect and diffidence.

'Mind you,' says Maureen now, matching up purple feathers with emerald satin to great effect, 'if I were Derek I'd certainly beat Erica to death. Fancy having to listen to that whining voice night after night. The only trouble is he's become too much of a gentleman. He'll never have the courage to do it. Turned his back on his origins, and all that. It doesn't do.'

Maureen has known Derek since the old days in Hoxton. They were evacuees together: shared the same bomb shelter on their return from Starvation Hall in Felixstowe – a boys' public school considered unsafe for the gentry's children but all right for the East Enders.

'It's all Erica's fantasy,' says Ruthie, knowledgeably. 'A kind of dreadful sexual fantasy. She *wants* him to beat her up so she trots round London saying he does. Poor Derek. It comes from marrying into the English upper classes, old style. She must be nearly fifty. She has that kind of battered-looking face.'

Her voice trails away. There is a slight pause in the conversation.

'Um,' says Alison.

'That's drink,' says Maureen, decisively. 'Poor bloody Derek. What a ball-breaker to have married.' Derek was Maureen's childhood sweetheart. What a romantic, platonic idyll! She nearly married him once, twice, three times. Once in the

45

very early days, before Kim, before anyone, when Derek was selling books from a barrow in Hoxton market. Once again, after Kim and before the professor, by which time Derek was taking expensive photographs of the trendy and successful – only then Erica turned up in Derek's bed, long-legged, disdainful, beautiful, with a model's precise and organised face, and the fluty tones of the girl who'd bought her school uniform at Harrods, and that was the end of that. Not that Derek had ever exactly proposed to Maureen; not that they'd ever even been to bed together: they just knew each other and each other's bed partners so well that each knew what the other was thinking, feeling, hoping. Both from Hoxton, East London: Derek, Maureen; and a host of others, too. What was there, you might ask, about that particular acre of the East End which over a period of a few years gave birth to such a crop of remarkable children, such a flare-up of human creativity in terms of writing, painting, designing, entertaining? Changing the world? One might almost think God had chosen it for an experiment in intensive talent-breeding. Mauromania, God-sent.

And then there was another time in the late sixties, when there was a short break between Derek and Erica – Erica had a hysterectomy against Derek's wishes; but during those two weeks of opportunity Maureen, her business flourishing, her designs world famous, Mauromania a label for even trendy young queens (royal, that is) to boast, rich beyond counting – during those two special weeks of all weeks Maureen fell head over heels classically in love with Pedro: no, not a fisherman, but as good as – Italian, young, open-shirted, sloe-eyed, a designer. And Pedro, it later transpired, was using Maureen as a means to laying all the models, both male

46

and female (Maureen had gone into menswear). Maureen was the last to know, and by the time she did Derek was in Erica's arms (or whatever) again. A sorry episode. Maureen spent six months at a health farm, on a diet of grapes and brown rice. At the end of that time Mauromania Man had collapsed, her business manager had jumped out of a tenth-floor window, and an employee's irate mother was bringing a criminal suit against Maureen personally for running a brothel. It was all quite irrational. If the employee, a runaway girl of, it turned out, only thirteen, but looking twenty, and an excellent seamstress, had contracted gonorrhoea whilst in her employ, was that Maureen's fault? The judge, sensibly, decided it wasn't, and that the entire collapse of British respectability could not fairly be laid at Maureen's door. Legal costs came to more than £12,000: the country house and stables had to be sold at a knock-down price. That was disaster year.

And who was there during that time to hold Maureen's hand? No one. Everyone, it seemed, had troubles enough of their own. And all the time, Maureen's poor heart bled for Pedro, of the ridiculous name and the sloe eyes, long departed, laughing, streptococci surging in his wake. And of all the old friends and allies only Ruthie and Alison lingered on, two familiar faces in a sea of changing ones, getting younger every day, and hungrier year by year not for fun, fashion, and excitement, but for money, promotion, security, and acknowledgment.

The staff even went on strike once, walking up and down outside the workshop with placards announcing hours and wages, backed by Maoists, women's liberationists and trade unionists, all vying for their trumpery allegiance, puffing

47

up a tiny news story into a colossal media joke, not even bothering to get Maureen's side of the story – absentee-ism, drug addiction, shoddy workmanship, falling markets, constricting profits.

But Ruthie gave birth to Poppy, unexpectedly, in the black and gold ladies' rest room (customers only – just as well it wasn't in the staff toilets where the plaster was flaking and the old wall-cisterns came down on your head if you pulled the chain) and that cheered everyone up. Business perked up, staff calmed down as unemployment rose. Poppy, born of Mauromania, was everyone's favourite, everyone's mascot. Her father, only seventeen, was doing two years inside, framed by the police for dealing in pot. He did not have too bad a time – he got three A-levels and university entrance inside, which he would not have got outside, but it meant poor little Poppy had to do without a father's care and Ruthie had to cope on her own. Ruthie of the ribs.

Alison, meanwhile, somewhat apologetically, had married Hugo, a rather straight and respectable actor who believed in women's rights; they had three children and lived in a cosy house with a garden in Muswell Hill: Alison even belonged to the PTA! Hugo was frequently without work, but Hugo and Alison managed, between them, to keep going and even happy. Now Hugo thinks Alison should ask for a rise, but Alison doesn't like to. That's the trouble about working for a friend and being only a nominal partner.

'Don't let's talk about Erica Bisham any more,' says Maureen. 'It's too draggy a subject.' So they don't.

But one midnight a couple of weeks later, when Maureen,

Ruthie and Alison are working late to meet an order – as is their frequent custom these days (and one most unnerving to Hugo, Alison's husband) – there comes a tap on the door. It's Erica, of course. Who else would tap, in such an ingratiating fashion? Others cry 'Hi!' or 'Peace!' and enter.

Erica, smiling nervously and crookedly; her yellow hair eccentric in the extreme; bushy in places, sparse in others. Couldn't she wear a wig? She is wearing a Marks & Spencer nightie which not even Ruthie would think of wearing, in the house or out of it. It is bloodstained down the back. (Menstruation is not yet so fashionable as to be thus demonstrable, though it can be talked about at length.) A strong smell of what? alcohol, or is it nail varnish? hangs about her. Drinking again. (Alison's husband, Hugo, in a long period of unemployment, once veered on to the edge of alcoholism but fortunately veered off again, and the smell of nail varnish, acetone, gave a warning sign of an agitated, overworked liver, unable to cope with acetaldehyde, the highly toxic product of alcohol metabolism.)

'Could I sit down?' says Erica. 'He's locked me out. Am I speaking oddly? I think I've lost a tooth. I'm hurting under my ribs and I feel sick.'

They stare at her – this drunk, dishevelled, trouble-making woman.

'He,' says Maureen finally. 'Who's he?'
'Derek.'

'You're going to get into trouble, Erica,' says Ruthie, though

49

more kindly than Maureen, 'if you go round saying dreadful
things about poor Derek.'

'I wouldn't have come here if there was anywhere else,'
says Erica.

'You must have friends,' observes Maureen, as if to say, Don't
count us amongst them if you have.
'No.' Erica sounds desolate. 'He has his friends at work. I
don't seem to have any.'
'I wonder why,' says Maureen under her breath; and then,
'I'll get you a taxi home, Erica. You're in no state to be
out.'
'I'm not drunk, if that's what you think.'
'Who ever is,' sighs Ruthie, sewing relentlessly on. Four
more blouses by one o'clock. Then, thank God, bed.

Little Poppy has passed out on a pile of orange ostrich
feathers. She looks fantastic.

'If Derek does beat you up,' says Alison, who has seen her
father beat her mother on many a Saturday night, 'why don't
you go to the police?'
'I did once, and they told me to go home and behave myself.'
'Or leave him?' Alison's mother left Alison's father.
'Where would I go? How would I live? The children? I'm
not well.' Erica sways. Alison puts a chair beneath her. Erica
sits, legs planted wide apart, head down. A few drops of
blood fall on the floor. From Erica's mouth, or elsewhere?
Maureen doesn't see, doesn't care. Maureen's on the phone,
calling radio cabs who do not reply.

'I try not to provoke him, but I never know what's going

50

to set him off,' mumbles Erica. 'Tonight it was Tampax. He said only whores wore Tampax. He tore it out and kicked me. Look.'

Erica pulls up her nightie (Erica's wearing no knickers) and exposes her private parts in a most shameful, shameless fashion. The inner thighs are blue and mottled, but then, dear God, she's nearly fifty.

What does one look like, thigh-wise, nearing fifty? Maureen's the nearest to knowing, and she's not saying. As for Ruthie, she hopes she'll never get there. Fifty!

'The woman's mad,' mutters Maureen. 'Perhaps I'd better call the loony wagon, not a taxi?'

'Thank God Poppy's asleep.' Poor Ruthie seems in a state of shock.

'You can come home with me, Erica,' says Alison. 'God knows what Hugo will say. He hates matrimonial upsets. He says if you get in between, they both start hitting you.'

Erica gurgles, a kind of mirthless laugh. From behind her, mysteriously, a child steps out. She is eight, stocky, plain and pale, dressed in boring Ladybird pyjamas.

'Mummy?'

Erica's head whips up; the blood on Erica's lip is wiped away by the back of Erica's hand. Erica straightens her back. Erica smiles. Erica's voice is completely normal, ladylike.

'Hallo, darling. How did you get here?'

'I followed you. Daddy was too angry.'

'He'll be better soon, Libby,' says Erica brightly. 'He always is.'

'We're not going home? Please don't let's go home. I don't want to see Daddy.'

'Bitch,' mutters Maureen, 'she's even turned his own child against him. Poor bloody Derek. There's nothing at all the matter with her. Look at her now.'

For Erica is on her feet, smoothing Libby's hair, murmuring, laughing.

'Poor bloody Erica,' observes Alison. It is the first time she has ever defied Maureen, let alone challenged her wisdom. And rising with as much dignity as her plump frame and flounced cotton will allow, Alison takes Erica and Libby home and installs them for the night in the spare room of the cosy house in Muswell Hill.

Hugo isn't any too pleased. 'Your smart sick friends,' he says. And, 'I'd beat a woman like that to death myself, any day.' And, 'Dragging that poor child into it: it's appalling.' He's nice to Libby, though, and rings up Derek to say she's safe and sound, and looks after her while Alison takes Erica round to the doctor. The doctor sends Erica round to the hospital, and the hospital admits her for tests and treatment.

'Why bother?' enquires Hugo. 'Everyone knows she's mad.'

In the evening, Derek comes all the way to Muswell Hill in his Ferrari to pick up Libby. He's an attractive man:

intelligent and perspicacious, fatherly and gentle. Just right, it occurs to Alison, for Maureen.

'I'm so sorry about all this,' he says. 'I love my wife dearly but she has her problems. There's a dark side to her nature – you've no idea. A deep inner violence – which of course manifests itself in this kind of behaviour. She's deeply psychophrenic. I'm so afraid for the child.'

'The hospital did admit her,' murmurs Alison. 'And not to the psychiatric ward, but the surgical.'

'That will be her hysterectomy scar again,' says Derek. 'Any slight tussle – she goes quite wild, and I have to restrain her for her own safety – and it opens up. It's symptomatic of her inner sickness, I'm afraid. She even says herself it opens to let the build-up of wickedness out. What I can't forgive is the way she drags poor little Libby into things. She's turning the child against me. God knows what I'm going to do. Well, at least I can bury myself in work. I hear you're an actor, Hugo.'

Hugo offers Derek a drink, and Derek offers (well, more or less) Hugo a part in a new rock musical going on in the West End. Alison goes to visit Erica in hospital.

'Erica has some liver damage, but it's not irreversible: she'll be feeling nauseous for a couple of months, that's all. She's lost a back tooth and she's had a couple of stitches put in her vagina,' says Alison to Maureen and Ruthie next day. The blouse order never got completed – re-orders now look dubious. But if staff haven't the loyalty to work unpaid overtime any more, what else can be expected? The partners (nominal) can't do everything.

'Who said so?' enquires Maureen, sceptically. 'The hospital or Erica?'

'Well,' Alison is obliged to admit, 'Erica.'

'You are an innocent, Alison.' Maureen sounds quite cross. 'Erica can't open her poor sick mouth without uttering a lie. It's her hysterectomy scar opened up again, that's all. No wonder. She's a nymphomaniac: she doesn't leave Derek alone month in, month out. She has the soul of a whore. Poor man. He's so upset by it all. Who wouldn't be?'

Derek takes Maureen out to lunch. In the evening, Alison goes to visit Erica in hospital, but Erica has gone. Sister says, oh yes, her husband came to fetch her. They hadn't wanted to let her go so soon but Mr Bisham seemed such a sensible, loving man, they thought he could look after his wife perfectly well, and it's always nicer at home, isn't it? Was it *the* Derek Bisham? Yes she'd thought so. Poor Mrs Bisham – what a dreadful world we live in, when a respectable married woman can't even walk the streets without being brutally attacked, sexually assaulted by strangers.

It's 1974.

Winter. A chill wind blowing, a colder one still to come. A three-day week imposed by an insane government. Strikes, power cuts, blackouts. Maureen, Ruthie and Alison work by candlelight. All three wear fun-furs – old stock, unsaleable. Poppy is staying with Ruthie's mother, as she usually is these days. Poppy has been developing a squint, and the doctor says she has to wear glasses with one blanked-out lens for at least eighteen months. Ruthie, honestly, can't bear to see her daughter thus. Ruthie's mother, of a prosaic nature, a lady who buys her clothes at C & A Outsize, doesn't seem to mind.

'If oil prices go up,' says Maureen gloomily, 'what's going to happen to the price of synthetics? What's going to happen to Mauromania, come to that?'

'Go up-market,' says Alison, 'the rich are always with us.'

Maureen says nothing. Maureen is bad tempered, these days. She is having some kind of painful trouble with her teeth, which she seems less well able to cope with than she can the trouble with staff (overpaid), raw materials (unavailable), delivery dates (impossible), distribution (unchancy), costs (soaring), profits (falling), re-investment (non-existent). And the snow has ruined the penthouse roof and it has to be replaced, at the cost of many thousands. Men friends come and go: they seem to get younger and less feeling. Sometimes Maureen feels they treat her as a joke. They ask her about the sixties as if it were a different age: of Mauromania as if it were something as dead as the dodo – but it's still surely a label which counts for something, brings in foreign currency, ought really to bring her some recognition. The Beatles got the MBE; why not Maureen of Mauromania? Throwaway clothes for throwaway people?

'Ruthie,' says Maureen. 'You're getting careless. You've put the pocket on upside-down, and it's going for copying.

That's going to hold up the whole batch. Oh, what the hell. Let it go through.'

'Do you ever hear anything of Erica Bisham?' Ruthie asks Alison, more to annoy Maureen than because she wants to know. 'Is she still wandering round in the middle of the night?'

'Hugo does a lot of work for Derek, these days,' says Alison carefully. 'But he never mentions Erica.'

'Poor Derek. What a fate. A wife with alopecia! I expect she's bald as a coot by now. As good a revenge as any, I dare say.'

'It was nothing to do with alopecia,' says Alison. 'Derek just tore out chunks of her hair, nightly.' Alison's own marriage isn't going so well. Hugo's got the lead in one of Derek's long runs in the West End. Show business consumes his thoughts and ambitions. The ingenue lead is in love with Hugo and says so, on TV quiz games and in the Sunday supplements. She's underage. Alison feels old, bored and boring.

'These days I'd believe anything,' says Ruthie. 'She must provoke him dreadfully.'

'I don't know what you've got against Derek, Alison,' says Maureen. 'Perhaps you just don't like men. In which case you're not much good in a fashion house. Ruthie, that's another pocket upside-down.'

'I feel sick,' says Ruthie. Ruthie's pregnant again. Ruthie's

56

husband was out of prison and with her for exactly two weeks; then he flew off to Istanbul to smuggle marijuana back into the country. He was caught. Now he languishes in a Turkish jail. 'What's to become of us?'

'We must develop a sense of sisterhood,' says Alison, 'that's all.'

Alison's doorbell rings at three in the morning. It is election night, and Alison is watching the results on television. Hugo (presumably) is watching them somewhere else, with the ingenue lead – now above the age of consent, which spoils the pleasure somewhat. It is Erica and Libby. Erica's nose is broken. Libby, at ten, is now in charge. Both are in their nightclothes. Alison pays off the taxi driver, who won't take a tip. 'What a world,' he says.

'I couldn't think where else to come,' says Libby. 'Where he wouldn't follow her. I wrote down this address last time I was here. I thought it might come in useful, sometime.'

It is the end of Alison's marriage, and the end of Alison's job. Hugo, whose future career largely depends on Derek's goodwill, says, you have Erica in the house or you have me. Alison says, I'll have Erica. 'Lesbian, dyke,' says Hugo, bitterly. 'Don't think you'll keep the children, you won't.'

Maureen says, 'That was the first and last time Derek ever hit her. He told me so. She lurched towards him on purpose. She *wanted* her nose broken; idiot Alison, don't you understand? Erica nags and provokes. She calls him dreadful, insulting, injuring things in public. She flays him with words. She says he's impotent: an artistic failure. I've heard her. Everyone has. When finally he lashes out, she's delighted. Her last husband beat hell out of her. She's a born victim.'

Alison takes Erica to a free solicitor, who – surprise, surprise – is efficient and who collects evidence and affidavits from doctors and hospitals all over London, has a restraining order issued against Derek, gets Libby and Erica back into the matrimonial home, and starts and completes divorce proceedings and gets handsome alimony. It all takes six months, at the end of which time Erica's face has altogether lost its battered look.

Alison turns up at work the morning after the alimony details are known and has the door shut in her face. Mauromania. The lettering is flaking. The door needs repainting.

Hugo sells the house over Alison's head. By this time she and the children are living in a two-room flat.

Bad times.

'You're a very destructive person,' says Maureen to Alison in the letter officially terminating her appointment. 'Derek never did you any harm, and you've ruined his life, you've interfered in a marriage in a really wicked way. You've encouraged Derek's wife to break up his perfectly good marriage, and turned Derek's child against him, and not content with that you've crippled Derek financially. Erica would never have been so vindictive if she hadn't had you egging her on. It was you who made her go to law, and once things get into lawyers' hands they escalate, as who better than I should know? The law has nothing to do with natural justice, idiot Alison. Hugo is very concerned for you and thinks you should have mental treatment. As for me, I am really upset. I expected friendship and loyalty from you, Alison; I trained you and employed you, and saw you through good times and bad. I may say, too, that your notion of Mauromania becoming an exclusive fashion house, which I followed through for a time, was all but disastrous, and symptomatic of your general bad judgment. After all, this is the people's age, the sixties, the seventies, the eighties, right through to the new century. Derek is coming in with me in the new world Mauromania.'

Mauromania, meretricious!

A month or so later, Derek and Maureen are married. It's a terrific wedding, somewhat marred by the death of Ruthie – killed, with her new baby, in the Paris air crash, on her way home from Istanbul, where she'd been trying to get her young husband released from prison. She'd failed. But then, if she'd succeeded, he'd have been killed too, and he was too young to die. Little Poppy was at the memorial service, in a sensible trouser-suit from C & A, bought for her by Gran, without her glasses, both enormous eyes apparently now functioning well. She didn't remember Alison, who was standing next to her, crying softly. Soft beds of orange feathers, far away, another world.

Alison wasn't asked to the wedding, which in any case clashed with the mass funeral of the air-crash victims. Just as well. What would she have worn?

It's 1975.

It's summer, long and hot. Alison walks past Mauromania. Alison has remarried. She is happy. She didn't know that such ordinary everyday kindness could exist and endure. Alison is wearing, like everyone else, jeans and a T-shirt. A new ordinariness, a common sense, a serio-cheerfulness infuses the times. Female breasts swing free, libertarian by day, erotic by night, costing nobody anything, or at most a little modesty. No profit there.

Mauromania is derelict, boarded up. A barrow outside is piled with old stock, sale-priced. Coloured tights, fun-furs, feathers, slinky dresses. Passers-by pick over the stuff, occasionally buy, mostly look, and giggle, and mourn, and remember.

Alison, watching, sees Maureen coming down the steps. Maureen is rather nastily dressed in a bright yellow silk shift. Maureen's hair seems strange, bushy in parts, sparse in others. Maureen has abandoned her hat. Maureen bends over the barrow, and Alison can see the bald patches on her scalp.

'Alopecia,' says Alison, out loud. Maureen looks up. Maureen's face seems somehow worn and battered, and old and haunted beyond its years. Maureen stares at Alison, recognising, and Maureen's face takes on an expression of half-apology, half-entreaty. Maureen wants to speak.

But Alison only smiles brightly and lightly and walks on.

'I'm afraid poor Maureen has alopecia, on top of everything else,' she says to anyone who happens to enquire after that sad, forgotten figure, who once had everything – except, perhaps, a sense of sisterhood.

Man with No Eyes

Edgar, Minette, Minnie and Mona.

In the evenings three of them sit down to play Monopoly.
Edgar, Minette and Minnie. Mona, being only five, sleeps
upstairs, alone, in the little back bedroom, where roses,
growing up over the porch and along under the thatch,
thrust dark companionable heads through the open lat-
tice window. Edgar and Minnie, father and daughter, face
each other across the table. Both, he in his prime, she
in early adolescence, are already bronzed from the holiday sun, blue eyes bright and eager in lean faces, dull
red hair bleached to brightness by the best summer the
Kent coast has seen, they say, since 1951 – a merciful
God allowing, it seems, the glimmer of His smile to
shine again on poor humiliated England. Minette, Edgar's
wife, sits at the kitchen end of the table. The ladderback
chair nearest the porch remains empty. Edgar says it is
uncomfortable. Minnie keeps the bank. Minette doles out
the property cards.

Thus, every evening this holiday, they have arranged themselves around the table, and taken up their allotted tasks.
They do it almost wordlessly, for Edgar does not care for

babble. Who does? Besides, Mona might wake, think she was missing something, and insist on joining in.

How like a happy family we are, thinks Minette, pleased, shaking the dice. Minette's own face is pink and shiny from the sun and her nose is peeling. Edgar thinks hats on a beach are affected (an affront, as it were, to nature's generosity) so Minette is content to pay the annual penalty summer holidays impose on her fair complexion and fine mousy hair. Her mouth is swollen from the sun, and her red arms and legs are stiff and bumpy with midge bites. Mona is her mother's daughter and has inherited her difficulty with the sun, and even had a slight touch of sunstroke on the evening of the second day, which Edgar, probably rightly, put down to the fact that Minette had slapped Mona on the cheek, in the back of the car, on the journey down.

'Cheeks afire,' he said, observing his flushed and feverish child. 'You really shouldn't vent your neuroses on your children, Minette.'

And of course Minette shouldn't. Edgar was right. Poor little Mona. It was entirely forgivable for Mona, a child of five, to become fractious and unbiddable in the back of a car, cooped up as she was on a five-hour journey; and entirely unforgivable of the adult Minette, sitting next to her, to be feeling so cross, distraught, nervous and unmaternal that she reacted by slapping. Minette should have, could have diverted: could have sung, could have played Here is the Church, this Little Pig, something, anything, rather than slapped. Cheeks afire! As well they might be. Mona's with upset at her mother's cruel behaviour: Minette's, surely, with shame and sorrow.

Edgar felt the journey was better taken without stops, and that in any case no coffee available on a motorway was worth stopping for. It would be instant, not real. Why hadn't Minette brought a Thermos, he enquired, when she ventured to suggest they stopped. Because we don't *own* a Thermos, she wanted to cry, in her impossible mood, because you say they're monstrously over-priced, because you say I always break the screw; in any case it's not the coffee I want, it's for you to stop, to recognise our existence, our needs – but she stopped herself in time. That way quarrels lie, and the rare quarrels of Edgar and Minette, breaking out, shatter the neighbourhood, not to mention the children. Well done, Minette.

'Just as well we didn't go to Italy,' said Edgar, on the night of Mona's fever, measuring out, to calm the mother-damaged, fevered cheek, the exact dosage of Junior Aspirin recommended on the back of the packet (and although Minette's doctor once instructed her to quadruple the stated dose, if she wanted it to be effective, Minette knows better than to say so), dissolving it in water, and feeding it to Mona by the spoonful though Minette knows Mona much prefers to suck them – 'if this is what half an hour's English sun does to her.'

Edgar, Minette, Minnie and Mona. Off to Italy, camping, every year for the last six years, even when Mona was a baby. Milan, Venice, Florence, Pisa. Oh what pleasure, riches, glory, of countryside and town. This year, Minette had renewed the passports and replaced the sleeping bags, brought the Melamine plates and mugs up to quota, checked the Gaz cylinders, and waited for Edgar to reveal the date, usually towards the end of July, when he would put his ethnographical gallery in the hands of an assistant and they would pack themselves and the tent into the car, happy families, and set off, as if spontaneously, into the unknown; but this year the end of July went and the first week of August, and still Edgar did not speak, and Minette's employers were betraying a kind of incredulous restlessness at Minette's apparent lack of decision, and only then, on August 6, after a studied absent-mindedness lasting from July 31 to August 5, did Edgar say 'Of course we can't afford to go abroad. Business is rock-bottom. I hope you haven't been wasting any money on unnecessary equipment?'

'No, of course not,' says Minette. Minette tells many lies: it is one of the qualities which Edgar least likes in her. Minette thinks she is safe in this one. Edgar will not actually count the Melamine plates; nor is he likely to discern the difference between one old lumpy navy-blue sleeping bag and another unlumpy new one. 'We do have the money set aside,' she says cautiously, hopefully.

'Don't be absurd,' he says. 'We can't afford to drive the car round the corner, let alone to Venice. It'll only have sunk another couple of inches since last year, beneath the weight of crap as much as of tourists. It's too depressing. Everything's too depressing.' Oh Venice, goodbye Venice, city of wealth and abandon, and human weakness, glorious beneath sulphurous skies. Goodbye Venice, says Minette in her heart, I loved you well. 'So we shan't be having a holiday this year?' she enquires. Tears are smarting in her eyes. She doesn't believe him. She is tired, work has been exhausting. She is an advertising copywriter. He is teasing, surely. He often is. In the morning he will say something different.

64

'You go on holiday if you want,' he says in the morning. 'I can't. I can't afford a holiday this year. You seem to have lost all sense of reality, Minette. It's that ridiculous place you work in.' And of course he is right. Times are hard. Inflation makes profits and salaries seem ridiculous. Edgar, Minette, Minnie and Mona must adapt with the times. An advertising agency is not noted for the propagation of truth. Those who work in agencies live fantasy lives as to their importance in the scheme of things and their place in a society which in truth despises them. Minette is lucky that someone of his integrity and taste puts up with her. No holiday this year. She will pay the money set aside into a building society, though the annual interest is less than the annual inflation rate. She is resigned.

But the next day, Edgar comes home, having booked a holiday cottage in Kent. A miracle. Friends of his own it, and have had a cancellation. Purest chance. It is the kind of good fortune Edgar always has. If Edgar is one minute late for a train, the train leaves two minutes late.

Now, on the Friday, here they are, Edgar, Minette, Minnie and Mona, installed in this amazing rural paradise of a Kentish hamlet, stone-built, thatched cottage, swifts flying low across the triangular green, the heavy smell of farmyard mixing with the scent of the absurd red roses round the door and the night-stocks in the cottage garden, tired and happy after a day on the beach, with the sun shining and the English Channel blue and gentle, washing upon smooth pebbles.

Mona sleeps, stirs. The night is hot and thundery, ominous.

Inflation makes the Monopoly money not so fantastic as it used to be. Minette remarks on it to Edgar.

'Speak for yourself,' he says. Minette recently got a rise, promotion. Edgar is self-employed, of the newly impoverished classes.

They throw to see who goes first. Minette throws a two and a three. Minnie, her father's daughter, throws a five and a six. Minnie is twelve, a kindly, graceful child, watchful of her mother, adoring her father, whom she resembles.

Edgar throws a double six. Edgar chooses his token – the iron – and goes first.

Edgar, Minette, Minnie and Mona.

Edgar always wins the toss. Edgar always chooses the iron. (He is as good at housekeeping and cooking as Minette, if not better.) Edgar always wins the game. Minnie always comes second. Minette always comes last. Mona always sleeps. Of such stuff are holidays made.

Monopoly, in truth, bores Minette. She plays for Minnie's sake, to be companionable, and for Edgar's, because it is expected. Edgar likes winning. Who doesn't?

Edgar throws a double, lands on Pentonville Road, and buys it for £60. Minette hands over the card; Minnie receives his money. Edgar throws again, lands on and buys Northumberland Avenue. Minnie throws, lands on Euston Road, next to her father, and buys it for £100. Minette lands on Income Tax, pays £200 into the bank and giggles, partly from nervousness, partly at the ridiculous nature of fate.

'You do certainly have a knack, Minette,' says Edgar, unsmiling. 'But I don't know if it's anything to laugh about.'

Minette stops smiling. The game continues in silence. Minette lands in jail. Upstairs Mona, restless, murmurs and mutters in her sleep. In the distance Minette can hear the crackle of thunder. The windows are open, and the curtains not drawn, in order that Edgar can feel close to the night and nature, and make the most of his holiday. The window squares of blank blackness, set into the white walls, as on some child's painting, frighten Minette. What's outside? Inside, it seems to her, their words echo. The rattle of the dice is loud, loaded with some kind of meaning she'd rather not think about. Is someone else listening, observing?

Mona cries out. Minette gets up. 'I'll go to her,' she says. 'She's perfectly all right,' says Edgar. 'Don't fuss.' 'She might be frightened,' says Minette. 'What of?' enquires Edgar dangerously. 'What is there to be frightened of?' He is irritated by Minette's many fears, especially on holiday, and made angry by the notion that there is anything threatening in nature. Loving silence and isolation himself, he is impatient with those city-dwellers who fear them. Minette and Mona, his feeling is, are city-dwellers by nature, whereas Edgar and Minnie have the souls, the patience, the maturity of the country-dweller, although obliged to live in the town. 'It's rather hot. She's in a strange place,' Minette persists.

'She's in a lovely place,' says Edgar, flatly. 'Of course, she may be having bad dreams.'

Mona is silent again, and Minette is relieved. If Mona is having bad dreams, it is of course Minette's fault, first for having slapped Mona on the cheek, and then, more basically, for having borne a child with such a town-dweller's nature that she suffers from sunburn and sunstroke.

'Mona by name,' says Minette, 'moaner by nature.'

'Takes after her mother,' says Edgar. 'Minette, you forgot to pay £50 last time you landed in jail, so you'll have to stay there until you throw a double.'
'Can't I pay this time round?'
'No you can't,' says Edgar.

They've lost the rule book. All losses in the house are Minette's responsibility, so it is only justice that Edgar's ruling as to the nature of the game shall be accepted. Minette stays in jail.

Mona by name, moaner by nature. It was Edgar who named his children, not Minette. Childbirth upset her judgment, made her impossible, or so Edgar said, and she was willing to believe it, struggling to suckle her young under Edgar's alternately indifferent and chiding eye, sore from stitches, trying to decide on a name, and unable to make up her mind, for any name Minette liked, Edgar didn't. For convenience sake, while searching for a compromise, she referred to her first-born as Mini – such a tiny, beautiful baby – and when Edgar came back unexpectedly with the birth certificate, there was the name Minnie, and Minette gasped with horror, and all Edgar said was, 'But I thought that was what *you* wanted, it's what *you* called her, the State won't wait for ever for *you* to make up your mind; I had to spend all morning in that place and I ought to be in the gallery; I'm exhausted. Aren't you grateful for anything? You've got to get that baby to sleep right through the night somehow before I go mad.' Well, what could she say? Or do? Minnie she was. Minnie Mouse. But in a way it suited her, or at any rate she transcended it, a beautiful loving child, her father's darling, mother's too.

Minette uses Minnie as good Catholics use the saints – as an intercessionary power.

Minnie, see what your father wants for breakfast. Minnie, ask your father if we're going out today.

When Mona was born Minette felt stronger and happier. Edgar, for some reason, was easy and loving. (Minette lost her job: it had been difficult, looking after the six-year-old Minnie, being pregnant again by accident – well, forgetting her pill – still with the house, the shopping and the cleaning to do, and working at the same time: not to mention the washing. They had no washing machine, Edgar feeling, no doubt rightly, that domestic machinery was noisy, expensive, and not really, in the end, labour saving. Something had to give, and it was Minette's work that did, just in time to save her sanity. The gallery was doing well, and of course Minette's earnings had been increasing Edgar's tax. Or so he believed. She tried to explain that they were taxed separately, but he did not seem to hear, let alone believe.) In any case, sitting up in childbed with her hand in Edgar's, happy for once, relaxed, unemployed – he was quite right, the work did overstrain her, and what was the point – such meaningless, anti-social work amongst such facile, trendy non-people – joking about the new baby's name, she said, listen to her moaning. Perhaps we'd better call her Moaner. Moaner by name, Moaner by nature. Imprudent Minette. And a week later, there he was, with the birth certificate all made out. Mona.

'Good God, woman,' he cried. 'Are you mad? *You* said you wanted Mona. I took *you* at your word. I was doing what *you* wanted.'
'I didn't say that.' She was crying, weak from childbirth, turmoil, the sudden withdrawl of his kindness, his patience.
'Do you want me to produce witnesses?' He was exasperated. She became pregnant again, a year later. She had an abortion. She couldn't cope, Edgar implied that she couldn't, although he never quite said so, so that the burden of the decision was hers and hers alone. But he was right, of course. She couldn't cope. She arranged everything, went to the nursing home by minicab, by herself, and came out by minicab the next day. Edgar paid half.

Edgar, Minette, Minnie and Mona. Quite enough to be getting on with.

Minette started going to a psychotherapist once a week. Edgar said she had to; she was impossible without. She burned the dinner once or twice – 'how hostile you are,' said Edgar, and after that cooked all meals himself, without reference to anyone's tastes, habits, or convenience. Still, he did know best. Minette, Minnie and Mona adapted themselves splendidly. He was an admirable cook, once you got used to garlic with everything, from eggs to fish.

Presently, Minette went back to work. Well, Edgar could hardly be expected to pay for the psychotherapist, and in any case, electricity and gas bills having doubled even in a household almost without domestic appliances, there was no doubt her earnings came in useful. Presently, Minette was paying all the household bills – and had promotion. She became a group head with twenty people beneath her. She dealt with clients, executives, creative people, secretaries, assistants, with ease and confidence. Compared to Edgar and home, anyone, anything was easy. But that was only to be expected. Edgar was real life. Advertising agencies – and Edgar was right about this – are make-believe. Shut your eyes, snap your fingers, and presto, there one is, large as life. (That is, if you have the right, superficial, rubbishy attitude to make it happen.) And of course, its employees and contacts can be easily manipulated and modified, as dolls can be, in a doll's house. Edgar was not surprised at Minette's success. It was only to be expected. And she never remembered to turn off the lights, and turned up the central heating much too high, being irritatingly sensitive to cold.

Even tonight, this hot sultry night, with the temperature still lingering in the eighties and lightning crackling round the edges of the sky, she shivers.

'You can't be cold,' he enquires. He is buying a property from Minnie. He owns both Get Out of Jail cards, and has had a bank error in his favour of £200. Minnie is doing nicely, on equal bargaining terms with her father. Minette's in jail again.
'It's just so dark out there,' she murmurs.
'Of course it is,' he said. 'It's the country. You miss

71

the town, don't you?' It is an accusation, not a statement.

The cottage is on a hillside: marsh above and below,
interrupting the natural path from the summit to the
valley. The windows are open front and back as if to offer
least interruption, throwing the house and its inhabitants
open to the path of whatever forces flow from the top to the
bottom of hills. Or so Minette suspects. How can she say
so? She, the town dweller, the obfuscate, standing between
Edgar and the light of his expectations, his sensitivity to the
natural life forces which flow between the earth and him.

Edgar has green fingers, no doubt about it. See his tomatoes
in the window-box of his Museum Street gallery? What a
triumph!

'Couldn't we have the windows closed?' she asks.
'What for?' he enquires. 'Do *you* want the windows closed,
Minnie?'
Minnie shrugs, too intent on missing her father's hotel on
Northumberland Avenue to care one way or the other.
Minnie has a fierce competitive spirit. Edgar, denying
his own, marvels at it. 'Why do you want to shut out
the night?' Edgar demands.
'I don't,' Minette protests. But she does. Yes, she does. Mona
stirs and whimpers upstairs: Minette wants to go to her, close
her windows, stop the dark rose heads nodding, whispering
distress, but how can she? It is Minette's turn to throw the
dice. Her hand trembles. Another five. Chance. You win
£10, second prize in beauty contest.

'Not with your nose in that condition,' says Edgar, and

laughs. Minnie and Minette laugh as well. 'And your cheeks the colour of poor Mona's. Still, one is happy to know there is a natural justice.'

A crack of thunder splits the air; one second, two seconds, three seconds – and there's the lightning, double-forked, streaking down to the oak-blurred ridge of hills in front of the house.

'I love storms,' says Edgar. 'It's coming this way.'
'I'll just go and shut Mona's window,' says Minette.
'She's perfectly all right,' says Edgar. 'Stop fussing and for God's sake stay out of jail. You're casting a gloom, Minette. There's no fun in playing if one's the only one with hotels.' As of course Edgar is, though Minnie's scattering houses up and down the board.

Minette lands on Community. A £20 speeding fine or take a Chance. She takes a Chance. Pay £150 in school fees.

The air remains dry and still. Thunder and lightning, though monstrously active, remain at their distance, the other side of the hills. The front door creaks silently open, of its own volition. Not a whisper of wind – only the baked parched air.

'Ooh,' squeaks Minnie, agreeably frightened.

Minette is dry-mouthed with terror, staring at the black beyond the door.

'A visitor,' cries Edgar. 'Come in, come in,' and he mimes a welcome to the invisible guest, getting to his feet, hospitably pulling back the empty ladderback chair at the end of the table. The house is open, after all, to whoever, whatever, chooses to call, on the way from the top of the hill to the bottom.

Minette's mouth is open: her eyes appalled. Edgar sees, scorns, sneers.

'Don't, Daddy,' says Minnie. 'It's spooky,' but Edgar is not to be stopped.
'Come in,' he repeats. 'Make yourself at home. Don't stumble like that. Just because you've got no eyes.'

Minette is on her feet. Monopoly money, taken up by the first sudden gust of storm wind, flies about the room. Minnie pursues it, half-laughing, half-panicking.

Minette tugs her husband's inflexible arm.

'Stop,' she beseeches. 'Don't tease. Don't.' No eyes! Oh, Edgar, Minette, Minnie and Mona, what blindness is there amongst you now? What threat to your existence? An immense peal of thunder crackles, it seems, directly over-head: lightning, both sheet and fork, dims the electric light and achieves a strobe-lighting effect of cosmic vulgarity, blinding and bouncing round the white walls, and now, upon the wind, rain, large-dropped, blows in through open door and windows.

'Shut them,' shrieks Minette. 'I told you. Quickly! Minnie, come and help —'

'Don't fuss. What does it matter? A little rain. Surely you're

74

not frightened of storms?' enquires Edgar, standing just where he is, not moving, not helping, like some great tree standing up to a torrent. For once Minette ignores him and with Minnie gets door and windows shut. The rain changes its nature, becomes drenching and blinding; their faces and clothes are wet with it. Minnie runs up to Mona's room, to make that waterproof. Still Edgar stands, smiling, staring out of the window at the amazing splitting sky. Only then, as he smiles, does Minette realise what she has done. She has shut the thing, the person with no eyes, in with her family. Even if it wants to go, would of its own accord drift down on its way towards the valley, it can't.

Minette runs to open the back door. Edgar follows, slow and curious.

'Why do you open the back door,' he enquires, 'having insisted on shutting everything else? You're very strange, Minette.'

Wet, darkness, noise, fear make her brave.
'You're the one who's strange. A man with no eyes!' she declares, sharp and brisk as she sometimes is at her office, chiding inefficiency, achieving sense and justice. 'Fancy asking in a man with no eyes. What sort of countryman would do a thing like that? You know nothing about anything, people, country, nature. Nothing.'

I know more than he does, she thinks, in this mad excess of arrogance. I may work in an advertising agency. I may prefer central heating to carrying coals, and a frozen pizza to a fresh mackerel, but I grant the world its dignity. I am aware of what I don't know, what I don't understand,

and that's more than you can do. My body moves with the tides, bleeds with the moon, burns in the sun: I, Minette, I am a poor passing fragment of humanity: I obey laws I only dimly understand, but I am aware that the penalty of defying them is at best disaster, at worst death.

Thing with no eyes. Yes. The Taniwha. The Taniwha will get you if you don't look out! The sightless blundering monster of the bush, catching little children who stumble into him, devouring brains, bones, eyes and all. On that wild Australasian shore which my husband does not recognise as country, being composed of sand, shore and palmy forest, rather than of patchworked fields and thatch, lurked a blind and eyeless thing, that's where the Taniwha lives. The Taniwha will get you if you don't watch out! Little Minette, Mona's age, shrieked it at her infant enemies, on her father's instructions. That'll frighten them, he said, full of admonition and care, as ever. They'll stop teasing, leave you alone. Minette's father, tall as a tree, legs like poles. Little Minette's arms clasped round them to the end, wrenched finally apart, to set him free to abandon her, leave her to the Taniwha. The Taniwha will get you if you don't watch out. Wish it on others, what happens to you? Serve you right, with knobs on.

'You know nothing about anything,' she repeats now. 'What country person, after dark, sits with the windows open and invites in invisible strangers? Especially ones who are blind.'

Well, Edgar is angry. Of course he is. He stares at her bleakly. Then Edgar steps out of the back door into the rain, now fitful rather than torrential, and flings himself upon his back on the grass, face turned to the tumultuous heavens, arms outspread, drinking in noise, rain, wind, nature, at one with the convulsing universe.

Minnie joins her mother at the door.

'What's he doing?' she asks, nervous.

'Being at one with nature,' observes Minette, cool and casual for Minnie's benefit. 'He'll get very wet, I'm afraid.'

Rain turns to hail, spattering against the house like machine-gun bullets. Edgar dives for the safety of the house, stands in the kitchen drying his hair with the dish towel, silent, angrier than ever.

'Can't we go on with Monopoly?' beseeches Minnie from the doorway. 'Can't we, Mum? The money's only got a little damp. I've got it all back.'
'Not until your father puts that chair back as it was.'
'What chair, Minette?' enquires Edgar, so extremely annoyed with his wife that he is actually talking to her direct. The rest of the holiday is lost, she knows it.
'The ladderback chair. You asked in something from the night to sit on it,' cries Minette, over the noise of nature, hung now for a sheep as well as a lamb, 'now put it back where it was.'

Telling Edgar what to do? Impudence.

'You are mad,' he says seriously. 'Why am I doomed to marry mad women?' Edgar's first wife Hetty went into a mental home after a year of marriage and never re-emerged. She was a very trying woman, according to Edgar.

Mad? What's mad in a mad world? Madder than the dice, sending Minette to jail, back and back again, sending Edgar racing round the board, collecting money, property, power: pacing Minnie in between the two of them, but always nearer her father than her mother? Minnie, hot on Edgar's heels, learning habits to last a lifetime?

All the same, oddly, Edgar goes to the ladderback chair, left pulled back for its unseen guest, and puts it in its original position, square against the table.

'Stop being so spooky,' cries Minnie, 'both of you.'

Minette wants to say 'and now tell it go away –' but her mouth won't say the words. It would make it too much there. Acknowledgement is dangerous; it gives body to the insubstantial.

Edgar turns to Minette. Edgar smiles, as a sane person, humouring, smiles at an insane one. And he takes Minette's raincoat from the peg, wet as he already is, and races off through the wind to see if the car windows have been properly closed.

Minette is proud of her Bonnie Cashin raincoat. It cost one hundred and twenty pounds, though she told Edgar it was fifteen pounds fifty, reduced from twenty-three pounds. It has never actually been in the rain before and she fears for its safety. She can't ask Edgar not to wear it. He would look at her in blank unfriendliness and say, 'But I thought it was a raincoat. You described it as a raincoat. If it's a raincoat, why can't you use it in the rain? Or were you lying to me? It isn't a raincoat after all?'

Honestly, she'd rather the coat shrunk than go through all that. Silly garment to have bought in the first place: Edgar was quite right. Well, would have been had he known. Minette sometimes wonders why she tells so many lies. Her head is dizzy.

The chair at the top of the table seems empty. The man with no eyes is out of the house: Edgar, coat over head, can be seen through the rain haze, stumbling past the front hedge towards the car. Will lightning strike him? Will he fall dead? No.

If the car windows are open, whose fault? Hers, Minnie's?

'I wish you'd seen that Mona shut the car door after her.' Her fault, as Mona's mother. 'And why haven't you woken her? This is a wonderful storm.'

And up he goes to be a better mother to Mona than Minette will ever be, waking his reluctant, sleep-heavy younger daughter to watch the storm, taking her on his knee, explaining the nature and function of electrical discharge the while: now ignoring Minette's presence entirely. When annoyed with her, which is much of the time, for so many of Minette's attitudes and pretensions irritate Edgar deeply, he chooses to pretend she doesn't exist.

Edgar, Minette, Minnie and Mona, united, watching a storm from a holiday cottage. Happy families.

The storm passes: soon it is like gunfire, flashing and

banging on the other side of the hills. The lights go out. A power line down, somewhere. No one shrieks, not even Mona: it merely, suddenly, becomes dark. But oh how dark the country is.

'Well,' says Edgar presently, 'where are the matches? Candles?'

Where, indeed. Minette gropes, useless, trembling, up and down her silent haunted home. How foolish of Minette, knowing there was a storm coming, knowing (surely!) that country storms meant country power cuts, not to have located them earlier. Edgar finds them; he knew where they were all the time.

They go to bed. Edgar and Minette pass on the stairs. He is silent. He is not talking to her. She talks to him.
'Well,' she says, 'you're lucky. All he did was make the lights go out. The man with no eyes.'

He does not bother to reply. What can be said to a mad woman that's in any way meaningful?

All night Edgar sleeps on the far edge of the double bed, away from her, forbidding even in his sleep. So, away from her, he will sleep for the next four or even five days. Minette lies awake for an hour or so, and finally drifts off into a stunned and unrefreshing sleep.

In the morning she is brisk and smiling for the sake of the children, her voice fluty with false cheer, like some Kensington lady in Harrods Food Hall. Sweeping the floor, before breakfast, she avoids the end of the table, and the ladderback chair. The man with no eyes has gone, but something lingers.

Edgar makes breakfast. He is formal with her in front of the children, silent when they are on their own, deaf to Minette's pleasantries. Presently she falls silent too. He adorns a plate of scrambled eggs with buttercups and adjures the children to eat them. Minette has some vague recollection of reading that buttercups are poisonous: she murmurs something of the sort and Edgar winces, visibly. She says no more.

No harm comes to the children, of course. She must have misremembered. Edgar plans omelette, a buttercup salad and nettle soup for lunch. That will be fun, he says. Live off the land, like we're all going to have to, soon.

Minette and Mona giggle and laugh and shriek, clutching nettles. If you squeeze they don't sting. Minette, giggling and laughing to keep her children company, has a pain in her heart. They love their father. He loves them.

After lunch – omelette with lovely rich fresh farm eggs, though actually the white falls flat and limp in the bowl and Minette knows they are at least ten days old, but also knows better than to say so, buttercup salad, and stewed nettles, much like spinach – Edgar tells the children that the afternoon is to be spent at an iron age settlement, on Cumber Hill. Mona weeps a little, fearing a hilltop alive with iron men, but Minnie explains there will be nothing there – just a few lumps and bumps in the springy turf, burial mounds and old excavations, and a view all round, and perhaps a flint or two to be found.

'Then why are we going?' asks Mona, but no one answers. 'Will there be walking? Will there be cows? I've got a blister.'

'Mona by name, moaner by nature,' remarks Edgar. But which comes first, Minette wonders. Absently, she gives Minnie and Mona packet biscuits. Edgar protests. Artificial sugar, manufactured crap, ruining teeth, digestion, morale. What kind of mother is she?

'But they're hungry,' she wants to say and doesn't, knowing the reply by heart. How can they be? They've just had lunch.

In the car first Mona is sick, then Minnie. They are both easily sick, and neatly, out of the car window. Edgar does not stop. He says, 'You shouldn't have given them those biscuits. I knew this would happen,' but he does slow down.

Edgar, Minette, Minnie and Mona. Biscuits, buttercups and boiled nettles. Something's got to give.

Cumber Hill, skirted by car, is wild and lovely: a smooth turfed hilltop wet from last night's rain, a natural fort, the ground sloping sharply away from the broad summit, where sheep now graze, humped with burial mounds. Here families lived, died, grieved, were happy, fought off invaders, perished: left something of themselves behind, numinous beneath a heavy sky.

Edgar parks the car a quarter of a mile from the footpath which leads through stony farmland to the hill itself, and the tracks which skirt the fortifications. It will be a long walk. Minnie declines to come with them, as is her privilege as her father's daughter. She will sit in the car and wait and listen to the radio. A nature programme about the habits of buzzards, she assures her father.

'We'll be gone a couple of hours,' warns Minette.
'That long? It's only a hill.'
'There'll be lots of interesting things. Flints, perhaps. Even fossils. Are you sure?'
Minnie nods, her eyes blank with some inner determination. 'If she doesn't want to come, Minette,' says Edgar, 'she doesn't. It's her loss.'

It is the first direct remark Edgar has made to Minette all day. Minette is pleased, smiles, lays her hand on his arm. Edgar ignores her gesture. Did she really think his displeasure would so quickly evaporate? Her lack of perception will merely add to its duration.

Their walking sticks lie in the back of the car – Minette's a gnarled fruit-tree bough, Edgar's a traditional blackthorn (antique, with a carved dog's head for a handle, bought for him by Minette on the occasion of his forty-second birthday, and costing too much, he said by five pounds, being twenty pounds) and Minnie's and Mona's being stout but mongrel lengths of branch from some unnamed and undistinguished tree. Edgar hands Mona her stick, takes up his own and sets off. Minette picks up hers and follows behind. So much for disgrace.

Edgar is brilliant against the muted colours of the hill – a tall, long-legged rust-heaped shape, striding in orange holiday trousers and red shirt, leaping from hillock to hillock, rock to rock, black stick slashing against nettle and thistle and gorse. Mona, trotting along beside him, stumpy-legged, navy-anoraked, is a stocky, valiant, enthusiastic little creature, perpetually falling over her stick but declining to relinquish it.

Mona presently falls behind and walks with her mother, whom she finds more sympathetic than her father as to nettlesting and cowpats. Her hand is dry and firm in Minette's. Minette takes comfort from it. Soon Edgar, relieved of Mona's presence, is so far ahead as to be a dark shape occasionally bobbing into sight over a mound or out from behind a wall or tree.

'I don't see any iron men,' says Mona. 'Only nettles and sheep mess. And cow splats, where I'm walking. Only I don't see any cows either. I expect they're invisible.'
'All the iron men died long ago.'
'Then why have we come here?'
'To think about things.'
'What things?'
'The past, the present, the future,' replies Minette.

The wind gets up, blowing damply in their faces. The sun goes in; the hills lose what colour they had. All is grey, the colour of depression. Winter is coming, thinks Minette. Another season, gone. Clouds, descending, drift across the hills, lie in front of them in misty swathes. Minette can see neither back nor forward. She is frightened: Edgar is nowhere to be seen.

'There might be savage cows in there,' says Mona, 'where we can't see.'

'Wait,' she says to Mona, 'wait,' and means to run ahead to find Edgar and bring him back; but Edgar appears again as if at her will, within earshot, off on a parallel path to theirs, which will take him on yet another circumnavigation of the lower-lying fortifications.

'I'll take Mona back to the car,' she calls. He looks astonished.

'Why?'

He does not wait for her answer: he scrambles over a hillock and disappears.
'Because,' she wants to call after him, 'because I am forty, alone and frightened. Because my period started yesterday, and I have a pain. Because my elder child sits alone in a car in mist and rain, and my younger one stands grizzling on a misty hilltop, shivering with fright, afraid of invisible things, and cold. Because if I stay a minute longer I will lose my way and wander here for ever. Because battles were fought on this hilltop, families who were happy died and something remains behind, by comparison with which the Taniwha, sightless monster of the far-off jungle, those white and distant shores, is a model of goodwill.'

Minette says nothing: in any case he has gone.

'Let's get back to the car,' she says to Mona.
'Where is it?' enquires Mona, pertinently.
'We'll find it.'
'Isn't Daddy coming?'
'He'll be coming later.'

Something of Minette's urgency communicates itself to Mona: or some increasing fear of the place itself. Mona leads the way back, without faltering, without complaint, between nettles, over rocks, skirting the barbed-wire fence, keeping a safe distance from the cows, at last made flesh, penned up on the other side of the fence.

The past. Minette at Mona's age, leading her weeping mother along a deserted beach to their deserted cottage. Minette's father, prime deserter. Man with no eyes for Minette's distress, her mother's despair. Little Minette with her arms clutched rigidly round her father's legs, finally disentangled by determined adult arms. Whose? She does not know. Her father walking off with someone else, away from the wailing Minette, his daughter, away from the weeping mother, his wife. Later, it was found that one of Minette's fingers was broken. He never came back. Sunday outings, thereafter, just the two of them, Minette and mother, valiantly striving for companionable pleasure, but what use is a three-legged stool with two legs? That's what they were.

The present? Mist, clouds, in front, behind; the wind blowing her misery back in her teeth. Minette and Mona stumble, hold each other up. The clouds part. There's the road: there's the car. Only a few hundred yards. There is Minnie, red hair gleaming, half-asleep, safe.

'England home and safety!' cries Minette, ridiculous, and with this return to normality, however baffling, Mona sits down on the ground and refuses to go another step, and has to be entreated, cajoled and bluffed back to the car.

'Where's Daddy?' complains Minnie. It is her children's frequent cry. That and 'Are you all right, Mummy?'
'We got tired and came back,' says Minette.
'I suppose he'll be a long time. He always is.'

Minette looks at her watch. Half-past four. They've been away an hour and a half.

'I should say six o'clock.' Edgar's walks usually last for three hours. Better resign herself to this than to exist in uneasy expectation.
'What will we do?'
'Listen to the radio. Read. Think. Talk. Wait. It's very nice up here. There's a view.'
'I've been looking at it for three hours,' says Minnie, resigned.
'Oh well.'
'But I'm hungry,' says Mona. 'Can I have an iced lolly?'
'Idiot,' says Minnie to her sister. 'Idiot child.'

There is nothing in sight except the empty road, hills, mist. Minette can't drive. Edgar thinks she would be a danger to herself and others if she learned. If there was a village within walking distance she would take the children off for tea, but there is nothing. She and Minnie consult the maps and discover this sad fact. Mona, fortunately, discovers an ants' nest. Minnie and Minette play I-Spy. Minette, busy, chirpy, stands four square between her children and desolation.

Five o'clock. Edgar reappears, emerging brilliantly out of the mist, from an unexpected direction, smiling satisfaction.

'Wonderful,' he says. 'I can't think why you went back, Minette.'

'Mummy was afraid of the cows,' says Mona.

'Your mother is afraid of everything,' says Edgar. 'I'm afraid she and nature don't get along together.'

They pile back into the car and off they go. Edgar starts to sing, 'One man went to mow.' They all join in. Happy families. A cup of tea, thinks Minette. How I would love a cup of immoral tea, a plate of fattening sandwiches, another of ridiculous iced cakes, in one of the beamed and cosy teashops in which the Kentish villages abound. How long since Minette had a cup of tea? How many years?

Edgar does not like tea – does not approve of eating between meals. Tea is a drug, he says: it is the rot of the English: it is a laughable substance, a false stimulant, of no nutritive value whatsoever, lining the stomach with tannin. Tea! Minette, do you want a cup of tea? Of course not. Edgar is right. Minette's mother died of stomach cancer, after a million comforting cups. Perhaps they did instead of sex? The singing stops. In the back of the car, Minette keeps silent; presently cries silently, when Mona, exhausted, falls asleep. Last night was disturbed.

The future? Like the past, like the present. Little girls who lose their fathers cry all their lives. Hard to blame Edgar for her tears: no doubt she makes Edgar the cause of them. He says so often enough. Mona and Minnie shall not lose their father, she is determined on it. Minette will cry now and for ever, so that Minnie and Mona can grow up to laugh – though no doubt their laughter, as they look back, will be tinged with pity, at best, and derision, at worst, for a mother who lives as theirs did. Minnie and Mona, saved from understanding.

I am of the lost generation, thinks Minette, one of millions. Inter-leaving, blotting up the miseries of the past, to leave the future untroubled. I would be happier dead, but being alive, of necessity, might as well make myself useful. She sings softly to the sleeping Mona, chats brightly to Minnie.

Edgar, Minette, Minnie and Mona. Nothing gives.

That night, when Mona is in bed, and Minnie has set up the Monopoly board, Edgar moves as of instinct into the ladderback chair, and Minette plays Monopoly, Happy Families, with the Man with no Eyes.

Holy Stones

He flew El Al, as befitted a guest of Israel. He would have flown first class, as he imagined befitted his age and his station in life – he was forty-one and a successful journalist – but flying El Al made that impossible.

The fact disappointed Adam but did not surprise him. That was the way, by and large, the cookie crumbled. Life, which gave with one hand, took away with the other. There was always something to mar perfection – a wart on a face, a flaw in a character, an uneasy grating, if not in a voice then in what that voice said.

'It seems there's not first class on El Al,' he apologised to Elsie, his new young wife. 'Israel has more important things to do than provide luxuries for the likes of us.'

'I don't mind,' said Elsie, happily. 'It just means we can sit closer together.'

And they squashed in beside each other and sat, knees touching, his and hers both in jeans. Elsie was twenty-three.

Adam's first wife Elaine, mother of his three children, had

long ago sunk into obsession and misery, and now they were divorced, leaving Adam with a sense of tragedy behind him, and solicitors' letters and bills still falling through the letter box. But the past was now finally redeemable – its events had, after all, led him to Elsie and happiness.

The plump girl in the seat in front of Adam stuck her little black high-heeled shoes out into the aisle. Her legs were bare, except for a thin gold chain around her right ankle. Elsie giggled at it and nudged Adam. 'Does that mean she's a prostitute? I never know.' Elsie had a double first in classics. No one would ever know that, either; at any rate not on first acquaintance. Elsie had large pale luminous eyes in a sweet, pale face, and pale silky hair, and a slight, slender body and long drooping fingers and a tender crotch. Adam loved to watch the shock on the faces of his friends as the girl they took to be Adam's latest lay turned out to be as bright as she was pretty, as aristocratic by birth as she was egalitarian in speech and manner, and as prepared to marry Adam as he was prepared to marry her.

Someone had told him, half joking, half serious, when he was alone and miserable and looking for love, after his divorce and before Elsie, that he was in fact too old to fall in love: that he would do better to draw up a check list of desirable attributes in a wife, and check off the girls he knew, and propose to the one who did best. No sooner had the check list been devised than he fell in love. Elsie would have come top, anyway.

The anklet girl in the seat in front was the kind Adam had loved to sleep with in the days when he searched for true love. White-skinned, small, plump, tottering about on

91

absurd heels – needing only a little dinner, a little push, and down they'd fall, on their backs upon his bed, awed by his station in life, the evidence of his column in the Sunday papers, their remembrance of his face smiling down from his advertising posters: their parts, in general, sweetly moistened by his position in the world as much as by his expert fingers. He accepted it. They didn't matter. In the morning, or even with any luck sooner, he'd say goodbye and mean it. Then the office. Then lunch with some girl he took seriously, whom he liked and respected and admired, and hoped to love; but somehow alas never did; and worse, felt too self-conscious, too judged, to take to bed without the presence of such grace. It seemed he was doomed to the half-sorry, half-exciting rites of lust.

But now Adam and Elsie. He had true love. And that was the end of philandering, of bachelor pad, of the calling of taxis at 2 a.m., of the hairpins and pants and scents that collected under his divan: of female tears alternating with female toughness, of the occasional parting with money – though mostly the pick-ups did it for love; a transitory love, of course, evaporating at the door, though deceptive enough at the time, for Adam had the talent of plucking out of the very air, or so it seemed, a sexual vigour which turned his soft lips hard and bruising, and blanked and slowed his usually bright and flickering eyes – as if he were the particular focusing point of some cosmic energy, predatory and fecundating, asserting its male right over the female. Girls who had been with Adam, however defended by pills and coils, worried lest they'd been made pregnant.

The anklet girl turned and caught Adam's eye. She had dark frizzy hair and a receding chin and slightly buck teeth, but her skin was white and her eyes large and beautiful beneath arched over-plucked brows. He wondered what she was doing and where she was going. There was a Christian tour on board, bound for Jerusalem, but the girls who belonged to that had the dull skin and dead eyes of the un-sexed. She could not be with them. He imagined she was Jewish.

What did the anklet mean? That she was someone else's property? That she was symbolically tethered? He did not know, any more than did Elsie. All he knew and cared, or so he told himself, was that now he had Elsie, whom he desired, admired, respected and loved, and needed no one else. He returned the anklet girl's smile, but coldly.

Adam pointed out to Elsie the armed security guard, posing as an ordinary passenger: a young man rather too strong and handsome for the shabby businessman's suit he wore. 'There's one or two on every El Al flight,' he told her. 'In case of hijacks.'

Elsie was impressed, frightened and reassured all at once. She grew pink and pale and pink again. She changed colour easily; he could read her feelings on her face. She was transparent to him. It made him happy, and safe from the fear, always with him, of being the object of mockery.

When the plane's engines roared, Elsie clutched Adam. She was frightened of flying. As it rose from the ground her hand left his arm and moved up to finger the little crucifix that hung from a thin gold chain round her neck. She had had it hidden beneath her T-shirt. Adam's happiness evaporated, and with it the feeling of safety, to be replaced by a sense of desolation, which he half understood and half did not, and the prescience of the end of love. 'I wish you wouldn't wear that,' he said, when the seat-belt light went off.

'It's only for good luck,' she said, and he bit back the retort that such a statement proved, if proof was necessary, the confusion in her mind between superstition and spirituality. Adam had a dislike of religions, both political and spiritual: he saw how faith in the irrational, how belief in the hero, had through the centuries led the self-righteous to murder, massacre and grief. 'It's not all that important,' said Elsie, raising her arms and with them her small, delicate breasts, and unfastening the chain. She stuffed the bauble into the pocket of her jeans. He felt happier again.

He hoped very much that Israel would teach Elsie a lesson or two as to the dangers of irrational belief. Adam's check list, finally drawn up with the help of Mrs Bramble – a painter of note and mother of six, who lived in rural confusion in Sussex, and whose talent and lifestyle were the frequent subject of articles on rural *haute-Bohême* in the smarter magazines – had not included a section on religion. That, in retrospect, had been a bad mistake. 'Now we must be honest,' Mrs Bramble had said, doing her best, pen poised over virgin paper. 'Brutal and dreadful but realistic. What do you require of a girl?'

'She must be attractive,' said Adam. The inquisition made him shy.

'What does that mean?'
'She must turn me on.'
'What turns you on?' Little by little Mrs Bramble bullied a firm description out of him.

Age: Under thirty.

Height: Two inches, or more, shorter than Adam.

Build: Slim, broad-shouldered, small breasted, long legged, with prominent pubis.

Colouring: Pale.

Eyes: Large, but not deep set.

Intelligence: High but not quite as high as Adam's.

She must play a good game of tennis, ski and swim and accompany him jogging.

She must turn brown not red in the sun.

She must not sweat under the arms.

She must be sought-after by other men: he must win her in the face of competition.

She must either be born to wealth or have achieved it herself.

She must come from a titled family or have achieved some measure of fame or notoriety herself.

'I'm sorry about all this,' Adam said to Mrs Bramble. 'It's just what turns me on. Does it sound ridiculous?'

Mrs Bramble held a baby under one arm and removed bread from the oven with her free hand. Hens walked in and out of the kitchen, picking up crumbs and pieces of food from the floor, which was just as well, as otherwise they would have stayed there for days. Five children fell upon hot bread, and divided it and devoured it, as might a pride of lions. Mrs Bramble wore an artist's smock, and a smear of fresh red paint was still wet upon it and coming off on the baby. She did her painting before the children awoke. 'Not ridiculous,' she said, doubtfully. 'Just rather specialised. There are so many different kinds of women in the world. I only hope you haven't limited yourself too much. What about her domestic qualities?'

'Just so long as she isn't like Elaine. Elaine was obsessively tidy. That was a real drag. But she must be a good cook and a competent hostess. I'm not looking for a housekeeper, don't think that. I want a companion, not a servant.'

'Fertile? Do you want that on the list?'

'I'm easy,' said Adam. 'I do have three already.' He seldom saw his children. Elaine was busy turning them against him. This, more than anything, made him bitter. He had loved his children, or so he had believed. But could such a one-way flow of emotion be termed love? Now he began to doubt it.

'I'm sure we're leaving something important off the list,' he said, but they could not think what it was, and there was an accident with the baby's nappy, and Mrs Bramble lost her concentration. Sometimes he thought that if only Mrs Bramble was ten years younger and a little less fecund, he could quite happily have married her – at other times not.

A week after drawing up the check list he picked up Elsie at a bookstall on a railway station. He'd thought she was a typist, or something like that. He'd been attracted to her at once, and fell into conversation with her, and when she agreed without demur to go out to dinner with him, had assumed she was some kind of prostitute. 'No,' she said simply, a week later. 'I just heard your voice and I'd known it for ever, and I looked up and recognised you as the man I was going to marry.'

Ah, it was a miracle. He thought that night, as he entered her, but I love her. And then, but how can I love a

96

cheap pick-up? And then again, as he felt, along with the accustomed surge of energy and relief, and the exercise of somehow punitive power, an overwhelming tenderness and happiness for himself and her – but I do! I love her, whatever and whoever she is.

He kept her the whole night and the next morning, and for lunch, and marvels unfolded. He discovered that her uncle was a peer and an aunt a millionairess, he remembered the mild scandal of the brief affair she'd had with married royalty at the age of sixteen. She had money of her own. She'd been at the station because she was running away from a long-standing, worn-out affair with a leading playwright, and had lost her purse.

She could swim, ski, jog, play tennis, cook cordon bleu, converse, was well-read but not as well-read as Adam; she was narrow rather than wide shouldered but he decided that after all he preferred that. He feared she might be cleverer than he was, but she laughed and told him not to worry. Hers was an academic intelligence – about the real world she was usually pretty stupid. She could not get from point A to point B without getting lost – which became to him a source of combined pleasure and irritation. She would lose her clothes, umbrellas, books and was untidy. He tidied up after her and was glad to do so.

Elaine had been untidy and cheerful to begin with, but over the years, little by little, had become obsessively orderly and distressingly afraid of germs. He sometimes thought that her progressive reluctance to make love had been a simple fear of germs. It certainly had not been the reason she gave in her divorce petition – which he had unsuccessfully defended

— that of his consistent infidelity. For one thing he had not — had he? — started going with other women until he had been driven to it, out of the sheer insistence of the sexual frustration imposed by his wife. Had she claimed her reluctance was because she was frightened of getting VD, he would just about have believed that. He took Elaine's jealousy as a sign that she did not really love him: jealousy, after all, betokened possessiveness, not love.

He hoped Elsie would be faithful to him, and certainly intended to be faithful to her: he could see that their particular brand of love depended upon sexual exclusivity.

They passed over the Alps. Elsie's hand lay in his. He squeezed it. 'Wear the crucifix if you like,' he said generously. She took it out of her jeans pocket and put it on again. He sighed. 'Religion is the refuge of fools,' he said.
'But I am foolish,' she said happily. 'You like me foolish.'
He could not deny it.
'How can someone as educated as you are, as sophisticated, believe in something so patently absurd as all that rigmarole?'
'Jesus isn't absurd.'
'Do you actually believe that Jesus is the son of God, was crucified, dead and buried and ascended on the third day and sitteth at the right hand of God the Father Almighty maker of heaven and earth?'
'I do! I do!' She giggled and laughed and seemed vastly amused.
'On the right hand? Not the left hand?' asked Adam, disagreeably.

'No. The Holy Ghost is on the left.'
'If he's a ghost he won't take up much room. They could both sit on the same hand.'

'You're silly sometimes,' she said, and looked quite cross, but not as cross as he did.

It was her wearing of the crucifix, when he first met her, that had persuaded him she was nothing but a cheap and superstitious tart: he had told her so later, and had thought she seemed shaken, and certainly hoped that she was. But still she wore it, from time to time.

And as the plane circled and lowered and landed, she fingered the crucifix again, and the hand which should have been in his was not and his heart sank, and he knew again that everything was lost. His mother had died when he was four; small incidents could still, suddenly and unexpectedly, bring back the overwhelming sense of loss, desolation and finality. He understood the feeling for what it was – as something which belonged to the past, not the present, and could not bear with it and deal with it, and wait for the pain to go away, as one might the pain of a stubbed toe.

He waited, and it passed. But he knew that though the symptom was cured, the ailment was not. The flaw had been discovered.

They travelled Israel in a minibus, in the company of other journalists, escorted by a kindly, elderly, cultured ex-ambassador. 'The country's full of them,' said Adam to Elsie. 'Israel believes in having its embassies everywhere.' In the more troubled zones their escort was a bronzed young army captain with a machine gun tucked under his arm, in the companionable way that such weapons are carried by their owners.

Elsie trembled under Adam's hand at the sight of that. Her colour came and went. Her fingers went up to her throat but he had taken off the crucifix in the hotel the night before, while making love, so now Elsie's fingers had to seek out Adam's hand instead.

He squeezed them, gratified. The anklet girl, surprisingly enough, was one of their party and a reporter from a Scottish newspaper. She could not be as stupid as she looked. Adam took care not to fall into conversation with her.

It was very hot. Elsie's skin was moist and cool. The anklet girl had wet patches under the arms of her creamy silk blouse.

'Such an energetic, practical country,' observed Adam. 'Israel pays lip service to religion, to keep its benefactors happy, but thank God it's not more than that. They've put all that superstition behind them.'

'Thank God they're not religious!' mocked Elsie, dancing round in the desert, stirring the glazed air, laying cool, hopeful lips on his. She would not take seriously his rage with the established religions of the world.

They went to the Dead Sea, where the sky and the land and the sea seem made all of the same substance, so that only the touch of the hand can determine which is which, passing through air, resting on ground, sinking in water.

They put on swimming costumes and bobbed up and down in the chemical liquid, which edged the surrounding rocks with white, like sugar frosting an iced glass.

'Like the beginning of the world,' said Adam. 'Well, this is the cradle of civilisation, after all.'

'I can see why they believed in Jehovah,' said Elsie, who was better at balancing in the water than was Adam. 'A great bearded face looming over the hills wouldn't seem at all out of the way. I'm sure He did loom, too.'

Adam's eyes smarted. He felt he was weeping though he knew he was not.

The anklet girl, coming down later with the rest of the party, declined to swim at all, but wore a bikini out of which her plump white body stirred and swelled, reminding Adam of times past.

They were taken to the Golan Heights, whence the Israeli army looks out over the Syrian plain and waits for attack. They crawled through dugouts and were allowed to use the giant telescope, which swept the desert and far, far away caught the glint of Syrian weapons. Nearer were the pretty white canopies of the UN tents, and the wreathed standards of the peace-keeping force, flying bold and high. 'It's been like this for ever,' said Adam. 'Armies of one kind or another, back and forth across the desert. It breeds paranoia.'

101

'The Lord God of Hosts is with *us*,' said Elsie. 'Can't you feel it in the air?'

Over dinner in Haifa Adam confided that he found Israel a distressing place. He had the sense of a culture being destroyed from within, and not, as it is thought, from without. The Arab Jews would outbreed their European compatriots and the sands of the desert would sweep back and drown art, and music, and books and learning. Civilisation. And superstition would rule once again over reason. 'I think it's the most wonderful country in the world,' said Elsie. They couldn't buy hot food in the hotel that day but only cold, it being the Sabbath. Adam was infuriated, Elsie entranced. She talked about the power of religious ritual, and the necessity of sacrifice.

They went to Jerusalem, that nexus of rare beliefs. In Adam's mind the yellow stones of Herod's temple – currently being excavated to a depth of twenty feet – were slippery with the blood of innocents. Jew killed by Christian killed by Muslim. The Canaanites and the Philistines, the Crusaders and the Saracens, the Israelis and the Palestinians, all bent on slaughter in the name of God.

Elsie peered down into the shadowed chasms of the excavation. 'To think that Jesus himself might have walked those streets!'

She looked up at the great lintel which marked the gates of the palace. 'And we know he passed under that!'

'Stones!' he ranted. 'Holy stones! You piled them up and down they fell, and you piled them up again, as monument to a different folly. But you used the very same stones, yellow ochre, spattered with blood.' His eyes were tired by the glazed yellowy look of everything his eyes fell upon. Sand, sky, or building.

They went to Bethlehem, where the Catholics, the Greek Orthodox and an assortment of other sects had their different versions of the birthplace of Jesus, and their own individual shrines erected, where hands could be best outstretched for the alms of the muttering dull-eyed faithful. Elsie blanched a little but solved the problem by going out onto the hillside of the Shepherds, holding her lovely face up to the serene heavens and saying, 'There in the East is where the Star appeared.'

She had even, in her first year at college, included astronomy as one of her minor subjects.

She insisted on stumbling up to Via Dolorosa, in the company of troops of murmuring Christian pilgrims and their greedy, ignorant guides. The journalists looked on from the safety of the bus. Adam was embarrassed. The pilgrims fell upon their knees, uttered incantations, wailed, rolled their eyes and moaned at the Stations of the Cross. At least Elsie kept on her feet and her lips closed. 'There's no historical evidence that these are the exact Stations of the Cross,' said Adam, 'even supposing these events took place at all.'

'Of course they did, silly,' she laughed, indulgently.

Little stalls sold religious relics of gross vulgarity and sentimentality which managed to combine the worst of

103

Victorian England, Renaissance Italy and contemporary New York. Adam said as much, and then felt himself turn cold as Elsie bought a brooch portraying the Virgin and Child, in gilt and orange and red and blue. 'Who's that for?' he asked. 'The maid?'

'I think it's lovely,' said Elsie, simply. 'It's a memento of a time when I was happy. I know it's in bad taste, but the Virgin has such a lovely expression on her face. Don't you think so?'

But he couldn't even look.

After the Via Dolorosa they went to the Wailing Wall. Tall pale men dressed all in black, with long ringlets beneath high hats and dark starry eyes, stood for long periods, faces only inches away from the wall at which they stared, and from time to time pushed folded pieces of paper into gaps in the stone. 'It's appalling,' said Adam. 'I suppose you realise Muslim houses have been razed to the ground to provide an open space so that those fellows up there' – and he pointed up to where an Israeli machine gun glinted on the battlements – 'can keep an eye on things?'

Elsie led him away from the Wailing Wall, where he seemed to get overexcited, and up the path behind it, and on beneath a sign erected by the Chief Rabbi requesting the faithful not to pass, lest by mistake they tread upon the Holy of Holies and defile it, and up into the sacred places of the Muslims, where the temple of the Knights Templar stood in white palladian beauty, welcome relief from the pervading ochre of sky and earth and stone, and there sudden and gaudy, in brilliant shiny ceramic, gold and crimson and vermilion, stood the great Mosque itself, burning in the sun.

The anklet girl followed them up the path. Her blouse was permanently marked with sweat. He thought he could almost smell her stench.

Elsie led Adam inside, taking off her shoes without demur, into the cool, domed sweetness within. There was, to his surprise, no altar, no pews, no aisle. The great circling vault existed to house a slab of stone – the kind that tops a hill, any hill. Smooth, sloping and important, as if set there by some almighty hand, but in fact merely left as the softer soil around was eroded by wind and storm, over centuries.

'That's the holiest stone of all,' said Adam bitterly. 'Where Abraham nearly sacrificed Isaac, or Mohammed rose to heaven, depending on which story you like to believe, and who owns it at the time.'

But she wasn't listening. He saw her fall on her knees, and with some difficulty, for there was a protective wrought-iron barrier between the object of worship and the worshipper, ease her long slender neck forward so that her lips could reach the stone. Then she kissed it.

Adam turned and caught the eye of the anklet girl. She stood behind him in the shadows, watching. He smiled, she smiled back. Soon he would manage to get her alone. She would not prove difficult. Half an hour's privacy, behind a holy stone or in a wadi or in some hotel room somewhere, was all that was required. He felt he needed the violence and relief of a new sexual encounter.

He thought he saw passing over Elsie's face, later on that week, the same expression as had come to mar his first wife's looks: softness hardening into sadness, gentleness into reproach, kindness into self-pity. He blamed Elsie for his loss of his love for her and he blamed Mrs Bramble for forgetting to put at least some stricture or other in regard to religion in the check list. His sense of himself as a tragic figure increased; he, who had been prepared to worship a wife, had married a woman who worshipped strange gods instead of her husband.

Threnody

1976/77

I don't want to take up too much of your time and attention, Miss Jacobs. I am sure there are many others in a far worse state than me. I met a couple of them on the way here, in fact, in the High Street. An old woman walked behind me shouting that Sainsbury's was the worst den of iniquity in the world and that the police station was a brothel. And a beautiful young woman passed me, weeping. Her face was so wet I thought for a minute it was raining. Well, I am in neither of those sorry states. I am prepared to take the world at its face value, and nothing distresses me very much any more. Look at me! My skirt and blouse are neat: my hair is combed: I am not distressed. I look what I am; a solicitor's wife, aged thirty-five, well set up for the slow run down to old age and death.

Depressed? No. I don't think so. Realistic, perhaps. Do I look depressed? I notice I am sitting in the bright light from the window, while you sit almost in the dark. I find that uncomfortable. I am not used to it. Usually the self remains obscure while others are brilliantly lit. Self-knowledge is hard to come by. That is why I am here. I want to say the things I do not like to say at home, for fear of making the milk curdle and the children anxious. I have blisters on my tongue, from biting words back.

Start at the beginning? Very well.

My mother named me Threnody. No. It isn't written on my card. I am known as Anne; well, who wants a name like Threnody? My husband Eric certainly does not. The name was a mistake on my mother's part. She thought Threnody meant some kind of happy, lilting melody. In fact, it means dirge, or lament. My mother's friend Elsie, who was to bring me up, pointed this out, but only after the deed was done. I don't hold the error against my mother. It was 1940, after all. Bombs fell and food was short, and I dare say she thought that Davis was a dull and ordinary surname, and that I deserved all the help I could get, and that was why she plucked Threnody out of the air, and used it for a name, instead of fishing Jane or Mary or Helen out of the common pool. And if more excuses were needed for my mother, she was only twenty when I was born, and my father was not available for consultation. What's more, according to Elsie, she had a milk ulcer. That helps no one think straight. I had one with Robert. He's my younger. And the Registrar would have been too busy entering deaths – Elsie said the week I was born was the week of the worst of the London bombings – to have had time or energy to help my mother out.

Yes. Elsie spoke a lot to me about my early childhood: yes. Perhaps I remember with her memory. See with her eyes. The world according to Elsie. We have grown apart for various reasons but I remain fond of her. I think those war years were the best of Elsie's life. She had three children and her husband was in the navy, and she lived next door to my mum and me, when I was a baby, in Riley Street. By all accounts it was a casual, slapdash street; a woman's world, for the husbands were away fighting Germany. Meals were seldom served on time, and came straight out of saucepans, not from serving dishes, and children shared beds with mothers and were the happier for it.

Yes, of course, Miss Jacobs. All these attitudes and assumptions of mine will be examined in the course of time. I know that and am prepared to change them. That's why I'm here. In the meantime I am just giving you the broad outline, so you know the kind of person I am. A solicitor's wife, burdened by the fact that her mother named her Threnody. A dirge or lament.

Where were we, before you interrupted? Though I must say you are very silent. I must be quite a good way to make money. Sitting there like a voyeur, saying nothing in particular, getting on with your knitting. Yes, a very good way indeed. I must try it some time. Set myself up so nice and cosy.

No. It doesn't make me feel better to have lost my temper with you. It makes me feel worse. Fourteen sessions before I was honest with you about my feelings? Is that good or bad? If it's neither good nor bad, why fucking well mention it? Can I now get on with my story, please? Christ, isn't that what I pay you for?

Riley Street in the war. Local schools had closed and such mothers as had stood out against evacuation now had the company of their children all day long. Bombs fell by night, of course, but quite a lot of the women claimed that air raids were preferable to their husband's attentions. According to Elsie. Yes. All this is according to Elsie. I was only a child, not Einstein. I do not have total recall.

Elsie wasn't like the others. Elsie liked sex. So did my mother. I don't think they were real lesbians, not in the modern sense. No, certainly I have no sense of disgust. Why should I? I can see it all clearly. The general feeling between them of a sensuous common bond; the slaphappy life of early nights and late risings, and cheerful neighbours and cups of tea, and time passing and no one caring, and mother-skin touching child-skin in the glow of the coal fire, and no one ever bothering to sweep up, and the money from the army coming through the letter box every week, so there was no hassle getting it out of husbands – and every night the bombers going over and real physical fear and the need for relief from it – well, I can see how all these things would combine so that Jan's and Elsie's lips were all but bound to meet, if only casually, and more in the expectation of comfort than in any actual desire for sexual gratification.

What do you mean, protest too much? I see that you're wearing a nice new jumper. Is that the one you've been knitting at my expense? You are not, if you don't mind me saying so, too good a knitter. You can't mind me saying so. I pay you not to mind.

Yes, I know that children like to deny their parents' sexual experiences; I have even heard my little Rosalind say Mummy and Daddy only did it the twice; once for Robert and once for me, and it made me laugh, though the way Eric's going these days, she wouldn't be so far out.

But for me, you see, it was true. I haven't mentioned my father much since I've been seeing you, for the I would have thought obvious reason that he died before I was born. He never even got to know I had been named Threnody. My mother wrote a letter to him and posted it, confessing all, but she needn't have bothered. He died before he could read it. He was on the African front. He was trapped in a blazing tank. No. Not a nice way to go. But that was the war. People got burned alive or asphyxiated or cut into bits or crushed flat or starved to death or died of disease: a nice clean bullet hole was rare. Killed in Action. If you disintegrated altogether and just weren't there any more you were posted Missing, Presumed Killed. They must have found bits of my father, I suppose. How do you mourn a father you never saw? He and my mother met, married and conceived me all in the space of two months, as was not unusual at the time. Then my father was sent back to the Front, buttons shining, leaving my poor young mother to cope.

I know it wasn't his fault. What are you implying? my difficulties with Eric are because of my father? My *father*? What father? Look, I don't have difficulties with Eric; he has difficulties with himself. What are you *talking* about?

No. That my mother had this relationship with Elsie is not fantasy. One day when I'm feeling strong enough I'll tell you how I know.

Poetry? Write poetry? Me? Do solicitors' wives write poetry? I suppose I wasn't always a solicitor's wife, though it seems hard to believe.

As a baby I had a transparent look – Elsie said so. My mother

111

didn't quite believe in my existence, according to Elsie, and that was the reason for my transparency. I think my mother was lucky: she was not quite able to believe in the desperate reality of anything. Why should she? She was Eve in the Garden of Eden, happy in Riley Street, until when I was four she bit into the apple of knowledge, and we were all cast out into outer darkness. Yesterday I sent a poem off to the Cheltenham Festival competition. I must be mad.

Talking about must be mad, I have to keep secret from everyone the fact that I come to see you. Eric says people will not just think, but know I'm mad, if they don't already. I expect he's right. He's always right. I married him because he was so right, and generally in charge. Never mind. Mustn't grumble. Elsie used to say mustn't grumble.

The apple my mother bit into was the apple of love. Had it just been sex no harm would have been done. Love doesn't just move mountains it sends them toppling down upon the innocent.

I don't want to come here any more. I can't afford it. I can't face it. It's doing more harm than good. My mother went dancing. She and Elsie had a row about it. I remember it. I was four. Elsie didn't want her to go. My mother had a pair of the new black glossy nylons and she put them on and Elsie called her names, but she went off to the dance and met a US serviceman called Gus and they fell in love. Gus wanted my Mum to put her past behind her, and that included me. Threnody. Dirge or lament.

I remember him saying to my Mum when she brought him home, 'Funny names you English give your kids,' and I remember Elsie saying, 'Not as funny as Gus. What's it short for? Disgusting?'

My Mum married Gus in Seattle and Elsie got one thousand pounds from Gus's family to take me in.

Sold to the nice lady next door. For the sum of one thousand pounds.

Well, Elsie was nice. Nicer than my Mum, I dare say. My Mum was a flibbertygibbet. The lady at No. 8 said so.

God, I feel about six. No, four. Christ!

1977/78

Historically, women have always abandoned their children in favour of their husbands. All through the days of empire, middle-class mothers left their little ones with nannies and schools and followed their men and thought themselves vir-tuous for doing so. Working-class women, of course, behaved more naturally. Perhaps my Mum was just being up-market.

Yes, I feel myself again. Surprisingly mature. I am runner-up in the Cheltenham Poetry Prize. Eric brought half a bottle of champagne. Had I won, it would have been a whole bottle. He's like that.

I remember when the war came to an end. Bells and flags and kissing in the streets. And then all up and down Riley Street husbands returned and children were pushed out of their mother's beds and lived for ever with a sense of Paradise

113

Lost. Meals became meat and two veg again: male voices demanded quiet and clean socks: and the pot plants began to flourish again. They do, I am quite convinced, in houses where normal sex is frequently practised. You are right: lately mine have been dying off. That's coincidence. Please let me get on, Miss Jacobs. Always butting in. If you're not too silent you're too talkative.

As for me, I belonged to nobody and had my own fate. Threnody. Dirge or lament. I had a little back bedroom at the top of Elsie's house and everyone was kind to me, and yes, I have always said I had a very happy childhood. I liked my name in those days. I was always good at turning misfortune into advantage. 'It's a Russian name,' I'd say to my friends. 'My father, who died the day I was born, was a prince. My mother was a princess. She was abducted by secret agents: she is imprisoned in a castle!' No. She never wrote to me.

I suppose in fact I was always a little ashamed of Elsie. I thought she was coarse and vulgar. I was very sensitive. I swelled up terribly if bitten by a wasp. I couldn't wear wool next to my skin. Remember the vagrant girl in the Hans Andersen story? They knew she was a princess because when she slept on a hundred mattresses she could still feel the pea underneath.

Ted? Elsie's husband? Ted my foster-father? Oh, Ted. Him. Well.

Elsie had another baby when I was eleven and Ted didn't like me very much in those days – I'm not surprised. If there were beans and chips I'd say isn't there any salad,

114

that kind of thing — and they needed my bedroom so Elsie wrote to my Mum, but the letter was returned Gone Away. My father's family? Elsie went along to the Registrar because all she knew, all anyone knew, about my father was his name, Arthur Davis, but the Registrar was gone with all his files. V2 rocket. Direct hit. That's war. People appear, and disappear, and history with them.

If anything goes wrong at home Eric says, 'Of course, you can't be expected to concentrate. You're a poet, after all.' It's all your fault, Miss Jacobs. Encouraging me to be something I'm not. I'd have thought you weren't supposed to do things like that.

I think I was a very pretty child. Well, that's the feeling I have. I loved nice dresses and button shoes. I remember Elsie saying, when I said I wanted to go to grammar school, 'Christ, that child gives herself airs.' But Ted backed me, surprisingly enough, and paid for my uniform without even complaining. He'd quite come round to me by the time I was thirteen. Yes, I was frightened of him. I'd wedge a chair beneath my door handle at night. No. I wasn't exactly frightened of him, more of the way Elsie didn't ever let me be in the room alone with him.

Anyway, Elsie was rescued from the threat of me by the government. They brought out a scheme for the residential education of war-disadvantaged children, so I was wrenched out of the grammar school where I was doing English Lit and learning to be a journalist and put into this institution and taught shorthand typing and office management.

Institution? Well, actually, it wasn't too bad. It was a stately home, which had been requisitioned from some ducal family in the war. Gold stucco flaked on to the filing cabinets and the canteen was set up beneath faded tapestries, and stone cherubs lay on their backs in the weeds and smiled. It suited my mood.

I slept alone in the servants' attic, beneath a sloping roof, and icicles formed outside my dormer window, but I knew it was better than Riley Street.

Yes, I made lots of friends at college. I entertained them. They were mostly very plain – being disadvantaged does tend to make people plain – and I felt in some way responsible for them. I always felt I had a future: but they only seemed to have pasts. They still write to me. One of them became a countess, for all her cross eyes. You can never tell.

Of course I see good looks as the way a woman gets on. Her face is her future. Would you be sitting there knitting shrouds – I assume you're knitting shrouds – if you hadn't been born with a face like a flat iron?

Flat iron? No, I have no particular association with flat irons. It just reminds me of your fucking face. Or vice versa. Look, I'm sorry. Yes, there's something coming up.

Ted. Foster father Ted. I learned office routine, book-keeping, shorthand typing. I'd given up wanting to be a journalist. You could be a secretary until you got married; but if you were a journalist that was a career. If you had a career you couldn't be married, and vice versa. And I wanted to be married, oh yes. I wanted to marry out of Riley Street for ever and into stately homes, however decayed. I settled for Eric, in the end, and Georgian country. Madness!

Love? What do you mean? Of course I love my husband. You're supposed to, aren't you? That's what it's all about.

Ted. Why do you keep bringing me back to Ted? It was better when you sat silent and gently snored; did you know you snored? – now I seem to hear your gratey whiny voice in my ears all day and all night. 'Ted – whine, sniffle – what about – whine, sniffle – Ted, whine, sniffle.' It was nothing. It was the kind of thing that happens to girls all the time. Ted came to visit me at the stately home. Stump, stump, stump up the wide staircase in brown boots. He was a good-looking man. Horrible, and old, and bristly, with a moustache. And angry, always. Not as if I'd done something wrong, but as if I *was* something wrong. Do you know? No, you wouldn't. You're always right.

Ted. He described himself as my uncle, and they allowed him up into my attic bedroom and he made love to me. Rape? I don't know. That's another word like love. I don't know what it means. I didn't want him to and yet I let him. I hated him and feared him and despised him and I wanted him to wrong me. He knew it was wrong, and I knew it was wrong, and he knew that I knew, and I acquiesced in this monstrous ugly act: I think perhaps it has made me passive. More passive than I need be. In order to accept that deed and incorporate it in my sweet vision of myself, I had to accept and incorporate everything else. The monstrous crime. Incest: in the spirit if not the deed. Yes, of course I'm rationalising, Miss Jacobs, whatever that means. If you'll excuse me

117

I'll leave this session now. I know it's early, but I'm sure your other clients are clamouring at the door. They always are. I'm surprised you can tell us apart. Perhaps you can't.

Why are you suggesting I start a business of some kind? I don't *want* to be independent. I think women should be looked after and it's the husband's place to do it. You know that.

Thank you. I had a good Christmas. I hope you did. Eric decided the turkey wasn't properly cooked, so everything had to go back into the oven, and it was all rather spoiled. Eric fears food poisoning. I don't. I hope for it. I have blisters on my tongue again. Haven't had those for ages. And I'm getting back pains.

Listen, I've got the premises for the Press, and raised the money for the lease. I'll print leaflets and wedding invitations, and circulars and handbooks and when I've managed to scrape together a little capital, even try doing volumes of poetry. I have quite a gift for handprinting, it seems.

I have been thinking about the Ted episode. He justified himself, as he adjusted his dress. Gentlemen were required to do that in public conveniences, at that time. Gentlemen will kindly adjust their dress. Meaning, don't forget your flies. He didn't. Some men make love without even taking off their trousers. Did you know? Well, you are *Miss* Jacobs. For all I know you're a virgin and have no idea what I'm talking about half the time.

Incidentally I have an Arts Council grant for the poetry editions. They needn't think they can dictate to me culturally, just because I take their money.

Ted's justification was that while he'd been away in the war Elsie had been having it off with my mother, so he owed her no fidelity. He thought a balance had been righted. And I'm sure he thought sex with me was his just reward for the money he had expended on me. Well, men do, don't they? But it was hit and run, really. He didn't write or phone and I was glad and I put it out of my mind, or thought I did. No. I felt no guilt towards Elsie. Should I have? But there has been a barrier between my life before and my life after; between my present and my past. I have become someone to whom the early life, the magic of infancy and total love, has been lost. I suppose that is how the traumatised live. Most of us are traumatised. Will knowing it make any difference?

1979

Miss Jacobs, I am in love. I shall tell you about it presently. A woman of 37 in love! Ridiculous. Heart pounding, mouth dry, loins melting. Oh! No. I shan't say any more about it. Not yet. Wonderful. I am so happy. Do you like my new jeans?

Eric. It was as much my fault as his. Now I am in love I can afford to forgive him. Look at my own part in it all. I was a tough little thing, really. After I left college I pushed my accent up a notch or so, acquired a fantasy Mummy and Daddy, and a country home and a horsy head square or two, and shared a Knightsbridge flat with a gaggle of secretaries who had all these things by natural right. Manners and attitudes brushed off. I meant to catch a man: the best man I could. I got a job with a firm of West End solicitors. I don't think anyone doubted me. I had the same clear honest eyes then as I have now. People believe what you say you are, if you say it loud and clear. So I did. Anne Threnody-Davis. Hyphenated. Madness!

Eric was the youngest partner in the law firm. Twenty-eight, unmarried, public school, private income, good background. There was, in those days, a very special kind of war between men and women. The woman's virginity was the trophy. The man's desire was to seduce the woman, prove her bad, and then abandon her as she deserved. The woman's was to snare and fascinate by sexual wiles, but exact marriage as the price of bed. Well I wasn't a virgin, was I, but I sure as shit tried.

Yes. My language has become freer. I think it's the company I'm keeping more than anything you've done for me. Freudian or sub-Freudian analysis doesn't go down too well in the circles I move in, I can tell you. But the Press is going very well. Do you think I should change its name to the Threnody Press? I'd like to do that. A kind of halfway acknowledgment. Eric won't like it, though.

I manoeuvred Eric into marrying me: sitting in his office as cool and sweet as could be, making up imaginary suitors for myself until he was so sick with anxiety and lust he proposed marriage. Once engaged, my various deceptions were quickly and horribly exposed. Served me right. I know I was a victim of a system which led women to weak survival by deceit but even so I behaved badly. I think Eric could have accepted Riley Street and Elsie and Ted with perfect equanimity if I'd been open and honest about it. But I was ashamed of it, and so he was too. He kept his word and married me but I knew he really didn't want to. He fell a third out of love with me when he discovered Threnody was my Christian name and not attached to Davis by a hyphen, and the second third when he actually made love to me on our wedding night and I confessed I wasn't a virgin, and the last third when we just somehow didn't get on in bed together, anyway. Look, I was only eighteen.

We both did our best. We lived in the country so I could put my past behind me, including the name Threnody. We had a nice house and nice children and I kept them both well. We entertained. I was a model wife. I went through all the motions; and we are always polite to each other. I felt so guilty about those initial deceptions that I thereafter behaved impeccably. But I died. I was dead. And even you couldn't revive me. Not so bad a crime? How can you say that? Think of the harm I've done! The damage. I killed my father: I drove my mother away; I stole poor Elsie's husband, I cheated my husband and my children of the life they should have had. You can say what you like to me. But that is the truth.

The truth of what I feel, not the truth of what happened, all right, but that is the greater truth and how am I to live with that? That I'm not just dirt: but poisonous dirt as well. I must be punished, obliterated. You know you have made me suicidal? Sheila says she hopes you know what you are doing. Sheila is the person I am in love with.

What's the matter? Why did you cough like that? Do you think you have failed? I *know* you have succeeded.

I don't think you meant to, mind you. But I know my true nature now. I am lesbian. I am going to come out. What is coming out? Don't you *know*? Where have you been the last few years? Coming out is declaring your sexual nature to the world. The theory being that if everyone does it, then straight society will stop being so censorious, and isolated gays will stop being so miserable, and realise what an ordinary, lovely, everyday thing same-sex-sexuality is. You might even start wondering about your own nature, Miss Jacobs. What do you mean, caution? No haste? God, you are so boring. Don't you realise I am in love?

Good heavens! Yes, ages and ages ago I said that. Sex isn't as dangerous as love. Mountains move and topple on the innocent. But I'm not deserting my children. Sheila is so good with them. They'll move in with us. It may be a bit difficult with Robert – I mean, he may be my son but he's still male, and male is the enemy, when you come down to it. But of course Eric will be reasonable when I tell him. We'll be so much happier apart. I really think he's a bit gay too, you see. People like me and him do tend to drift together, Sheila says.

Sheila says a lot, as Elsie did? What are you implying? No, I don't think so. In fact, Sheila doesn't believe in small talk. She's quite tall; nearly six foot, and really striking looking. She has a sort of husky, languorous voice. It really turns me on. I was publishing the newsletter for the lesbian commune she runs – well, she doesn't run it; it's a group thing: no male hierarchical organisation.

What do you mean, the world according to Sheila? As it used to be the world according to Elsie? What are you

122

trying to *say*? You're jealous. I think you're jealous because I'm happy and you're not. Yes, I know about my outer shell. My carapace. Sheila says all women married to men grow them, in self defence. We must use our sisters to help crack the shell, Sheila says, so the true self can emerge.

How much money have I given you, over the years? When I think how it could have helped the commune! You know the trouble I was having with the back? Sheila says it's because I've been playing heterosexual. She says she dare say if she submitted to male sexual aggression nightly she'd have a bad back too. Not *nightly*? Well, all right. You have a funny air, Miss Jacobs, crouched in your dark corner, of being girded for battle. Yes, I do see all male sex as assault, frankly. No, not an expression of love. Love between men and women can't be the love between equals, because men believe women are their inferiors. They can't help it. It's in the language. He before she. *Man* kind. *His*-story, John and Mary. The love men show towards women is at its best patronising. The penis is after all a weapon of mastery. Good heavens, look at rockets. Missiles. Whee! What a humdinger of an ejaculation! Wow.

I'm afraid Eric isn't being co-operative at all. He's being vindictive. Sheila says gays are, if they're under cover.

Sex with Sheila. It's wonderful. How can I explain to you? Peaceful. There is so much time. No fear of the other's failure, which will later be revenged. No fear of your own. Everything waits. The seasons. The earth in its orbit. Everything. It's love, as I have never known it. Eric won't give me a divorce. He has thrown me out. Well, he's a solicitor. He has friends. He is claiming custody of the children. He will only let me see them in the presence of a third party. Specifically not Sheila! It's barbaric, monstrous! Male vengeance. The man whose pride has been injured. That's all it is. Not *feeling*.

But I have the Threnody Press, which is just about now breaking even, and I have Sheila. I have no savings, no house, no children, no possessions: and many of my friends don't understand the truth and have taken Eric's side: but a few understand. Especially Paula. She's very supportive. And I have my dignity, and I have love, and when I have recovered from these blows, I will be happy. I am very calm, and very confident.

They are so kind to us at the commune. My sisters. Sheila and I have our own room: we're not in the dormitories. There are a lot of things I have to get used to. It is good of you to let me see you for nothing, even though it is only once a week. I would have thought, considering – well, never mind. You live as a woman in the old male world – you have to have your props. Money, status, possessions. We're different. Even our clothing we have in common.

Sheila has moved back into the dormitory. We talked it out. She feels there is something destructive in our exclusiveness. I see what she means. I think. No, I'm not depressed. It's just I haven't had time to mend my sandal thongs.

Of course it's a feather in Sheila's cap to have seduced a married woman with children. It's happening all the time. All over the country women are realising their true natures, coming out, leaving husband and children. It's nothing to do with fashion. If we are strong, if we hold together, as sisters, all will be well –

What do you mean, I use words without meaning? Miss Jacobs, I think I am going mad. Eric owns half the Threnody Press. He says I may keep it if I buy out his share. But that's two thousand pounds. I haven't got it. It will have to be sold. I am destroyed.

Miss Jacobs, Sheila says that emotions are political. That I should hand mine over to the group for discussion and direction, and not to you. But I don't know. I do love Sheila. I'm sure I do. I must, mustn't I? I mean, that's what's supposed to happen. Now when did I say that before? Round and round: circles within circles, little wheels within big wheels. Cogs grinding. Dear God, forgive me my sins.

Miss Jacobs, I met Paula in the street. I thought she was a good friend, even though she was heterosexual, but she was getting a bit funny and I asked her straight out why, and she said it's not that she thought it was disgusting or anything like that: just that she couldn't trust me any more. She couldn't relax in my company. She said it was as if I were one of the men, weighing her up for her attractiveness or otherwise, dismissing her because of her body, not her self. As if I would! But it's true that now when I look at the lips of women I wonder what kissing them would be like.

No. Pre-Sheila, I never had thoughts like that.

Do you mind if I cry? Sheila doesn't like me crying, and I have blisters on my tongue again. Why do I cry? Because of the children. Sheila says why shouldn't Eric take care of them for a change: much as she liked them they were something of a nuisance: it was difficult to be properly sexually spontaneous when kids were around. I remarked that heterosexuals waited 'til they'd gone to bed, and Sheila said yes, and look how miserable they are!

No. I don't see eye to eye with Sheila all the time, not any more. I think that's your fault. Eric has custody of the children. The case has been taken up by the Society for Lesbian Mothers. There's been a lot of press about, and even television interviews. God, I did look a mess. I'd no idea. Anyway, now everyone knows. Everyone. If I even put my head out of the door people stare.

It all reminds me of Ted, I don't know why. Stump, stump, stump, up the stairs, dreadful but inevitable. My doom.

My name is Threnody. It means dirge or lament. My mother didn't make a mistake. She had a foreknowledge, that's all.

Sheila wants Ellen to be included in our relationship. Ellen's twenty-two. Sheila says I've been a real drag lately, miserable and depressing and self-centred and unable to break out of my sexist conditioning, so that she's sometimes wondered if I weren't just a heterosexual playing sick fashionable games. I cried, which really made her angry, but the blisters on my tongue have gone. She said Rose Ellen would be good for all of us, being cheerful and positive – twenty-two, is what I think she means – and a bit confused politically, Sheila says, but fantastic in bed! Well, she should know. What does that mean anyway? Good in bed! She said to me Threnody by name, and Threnody by nature. A real drag, Sheila said. The world according to Sheila.

I accept that. Threnody. I fully accept my name. What did I do about Rose Ellen? I packed my one suitcase, which is all I have left of my life, and I went out into the world. Rose Ellen is *not* fantastic in bed: or at any rate she doesn't turn me on in the least, and she is very, very stupid. I have the suitcase in your waiting room. I shall go and stay with Paula if she'll have me now. You wanted me punished, I seem to remember. You didn't? It was what *I* wanted? Are you sure? I certainly feel much better. I mean quite dreadful, as befits my circumstance, which is totally ruined, everything lost: but nothing on either side of that, except a most wonderful cheerfulness. I shan't see you now for some time. I can't afford you. I mean, emotionally afford *not* paying for you, if you see what I mean. No, frankly, I don't think I have manoeuvred this whole situation just to get out of treatment. Goodbye, and thank you. I mean really, thank you from the bleeding, beating heart of Threnody.

1980

I see you have some new knitting. I love the colours. Much brighter! I hope it wasn't me who depressed you? I was going to post you the money I owe you but Tim said why not come and visit you and do it in person. I said you'd probably not be able to find the time to fit me in, but he said of course you would and he was right. Tim is often right, but not always, the way Eric was. Did I tell you about Tim? I don't know if seeing you did me the slightest good: perhaps all that was required was for me to meet the right person? Tim is a doctor. He was a widower when I met him. Now he is married to me. We have five children between us. Three of his and two of mine. Mine come at weekends. I am quite good friends with Eric now. He married again very soon after the divorce – a local farmer's daughter. Perhaps he was never the snob I thought he was, and it was me all the time? But since this is a social visit and I'm not paying you, I don't suppose you'll see the need to go into all that. In any case Tim likes me as I am and does not see the need for alteration. Do you know what he said to me the other day? He said, 'Don't tell me your mother made a mistake when she called you Threnody. She didn't. So far as I am concerned,' said Tim, 'the word Threnody now means a happy, lilting melody, and not dirge, or lament, at all.'

So you see, Miss Jacobs, all is well. What did you say? Nothing is ever as good as one hopes, or as bad as one fears? What a very sort of *intermediate* remark.

Angel, All Innocence

There is a certain kind of unhappiness, experienced by a certain kind of woman married to a certain kind of man, which is timeless: outrunning centuries, interweaving generations, perpetuating itself from mother to daughter, feeding off the wet eyes of the puzzled girl, gaining fresh strength from the dry eyes of the old woman she will become – who, looking back on her past, remembers nothing of love except tears and the pain in the heart which must be endured, in silence, in case the heart stops altogether.

Better for it to stop, now.

Angel, waking in the night, hears sharp footsteps in the empty attic above and wants to wake Edward. She moves her hand to do so, but then stills it for fear of making him angry. Easier to endure in the night the nightmare terror of ghosts than the daylong silence of Edward's anger.

The footsteps, little and sharp, run from a point above the double bed in which Angel and Edward lie, she awake, he sleeping, to a point somewhere above the chest of drawers by the door; they pause briefly, then run back again, tap-tap, clickety-click. There comes another pause and the sound of pulling and shuffling across the floor; and then the sequence repeats itself, once, twice. Silence. The proper unbroken silence of the night.

Too real, too clear, for ghosts. The universe is not magic. Everything has an explanation. Rain, perhaps? Hardly. Angel can see the moon shine through the drawn blind, and rain does not fall on moonlit nights. Perhaps, then, the rain of past days collected in some blocked gutter, to finally splash through on to the rolls of wallpaper and pots of paint on the attic floor, sounding like footsteps through some trick of domestic acoustics. Surely! Angel and Edward have not been living in the house for long. The attic is still unpainted, and old plaster drops from disintegrating laths. Edward will get round to it sooner or later. He prides himself on his craftsman's skills, and Angel, a year married, has learned to wait and admire, subduing impatience in herself. Edward is a painter – of pictures, not houses – and not long out of art school, where he won many prizes. Angel is the lucky girl he has loved and married. Angel's father paid for the remote country house, where now they live in solitude and where Edward can develop his talents, undisturbed by the ugliness of the city, with Angel, his inspiration, at his side. Edward, as it happened, consented to the gift unwillingly, and for Angel's sake rather than his own. Angel's father Terry writes thrillers and settled a large sum upon his daughter in her childhood, thus avoiding death duties and the anticipated gift tax. Angel kept the fact hidden from Edward until after they were married. He'd thought her an ordinary girl about Chelsea, sometime secretary, sometime barmaid, sometime artist's model.

Angel, between jobs, did indeed take work as an artist's

model. That was how Edward first clapped eyes upon her; Angel, all innocence, sitting nude upon her plinth, fair curly hair glinting under strong lights, large eyes closed beneath stretched blue-veined lids, strong breasts pointed upwards, stubby pale brush irritatingly and coyly hidden behind an angle of thigh that both gave Angel cramps and spoiled the pose for the students. So they said.

'If you're going to be an exhibitionist,' as Edward complained to her later in the coffee bar, 'at least don't be coy about it.' He took her home to his pad, that handsome, dark-eyed, smiling young man, and wooed her with a nostalgic Sinatra record left behind by its previous occupant; half mocking, half sincere, he sang love words into her pearly ear, his warm breath therein stirring her imagination, and the gentle occasional nip of his strong teeth in its flesh promising passion and pain beyond belief. Angel would not take off her clothes for him: he became angry and sent her home in a taxi without her fare. She borrowed from her flatmate at the other end. She cried all night, and the next day, sitting naked on her plinth, had such swollen eyelids as to set a student or two scratching away to amend the previous day's work. But she lowered her thigh, as a gesture of submission, and felt a change in the studio ambience from chilly spite to warm approval, and she knew Edward had forgiven her. Though she offered herself to multitudes, Edward had forgiven her.

'I don't mind you being an exhibitionist,' Edward said to her in the coffee bar, 'in fact that rather turns me on, but I do mind you being coy. You have a lot to learn, Angel.' By that time Angel's senses were so aroused, her limbs so languid with desire, her mind so besotted with his image,

131

that she would have done whatever Edward wished, in public or in private. But he rose and left the coffee bar, leaving her to pay the bill.

Angel cried a little, and was comforted by and went home with Edward's friend Tom, and even went to bed with him, which made her feel temporarily better, but which she was to regret for ever.

'I don't mind you being a whore,' Edward said before the next studio session, 'but can't you leave my friends alone?'

It was a whole seven days of erotic torment for Angel before Edward finally spent the night with her: by that time her thigh hung loosely open in the studio. Let anyone see. Anyone. She did not care. The job was coming to an end anyway. Her new one as secretary in a solicitor's office began on the following Monday. In the nick of time, just as she began to think that life and love were over, Edward brought her back to their remembrance. 'I love you,' he murmured in Angel's ear. 'Exhibitionist slut, typist, I don't care. I still love you.'

Tap-tap, go the footsteps above, starting off again: clickety-click. Realer than real. No, water never sounded like that. What then? Rats? No. Rats scutter and scamper and scrape. There were rats in the barn in which Angel and Edward spent a camping holiday together. Their tent had blown away: they'd been forced to take refuge in the barn. All four of them. Edward, Angel, Tom and his new girlfriend Ray. Angel missed Edward one night after they all stumbled back from the pub to the barn, and searching for him in the long grass beneath an oak tree, found him in tight embrace with Ray.

'Don't tell me you're hysterical as well as everything else,' complained Edward. 'You're certainly irrational. You went to bed with Tom, after all.'

'But that was before.'

Ah, before, so much before. Before the declarations of love, the abandoning of all defence, all prudence, the surrendering of common sense to faith, the parcelling up and handing over of the soul into apparent safe-keeping. And if the receiving hands part, the trusted fingers lose their grip, by accident or by design, why then, one's better dead.

Edward tossed his Angel's soul into the air and caught it with his casual hands.

'But if it makes you jealous,' he said, 'why I won't . . . Do you want to marry me? Is that it? Would it make you happier?'

What would it look like when they came to write his biography? Edward Holst, the famous painter, married at the age of twenty-four – to what? Artist's model, barmaid, secretary, crime-writer's daughter? Or exhibitionist, whore, hysteric? Take your choice. Whatever makes the reader happiest, explains the artist in the simplest terms, makes the most successful version of a life. Crude strokes and all.

'Edward likes to keep his options open,' said Tom, but would not explain his remark any further. He and Ray were witnesses at the secular wedding ceremony. Angel thought she saw Edward nip Ray's ear as they

133

all formally kissed afterwards, then thought she must have imagined it.

This was his overture of love: turning to Angel in the dark warmth of the marriage bed, Edward's teeth would seek her ear and nibble the tender flesh, while his hand travelled down to open her thighs. Angel never initiated their lovemaking. No. Angel waited, patiently. She had tried once or twice, in the early days, letting her hand roam over his sleeping body, but Edward not only failed to respond, but was thereafter cold to her for days on end, sleeping carefully on his side of the bed, until her penance was paid and he lay warm against her again.

Edward's love made flowers bloom, made the house rich and warm, made water taste like wine. Edward, happy, surrounded Angel with smiles and soft encouragement. He held her soul with steady hands. Edward's anger came unexpectedly, out of nowhere, or nowhere that Angel could see. Yesterday's permitted remark, forgiven fault, was today's outrage. To remark on the weather to break an uneasy silence, might be seen as evidence of a complaining nature: to be reduced to tears by his first unexpected biting remark, further fuel for his grievance.

Edward, in such moods, would go to his studio and lock the door, and though Angel (soon learning that to weep outside the door or beat against it, moaning and crying and protesting, would merely prolong his anger and her torment) would go out to the garden and weed or dig or plant as if nothing were happening, would feel Edward's anger seeping out from under the door, darkening the sun, poisoning the earth; or at any rate spoiling her fingers in relation to the earth, so that they trembled and made mistakes and nothing grew.

The blind shakes. The moon goes behind a cloud. Tap, tap, overhead. Back and forth. The wind? No. Don't delude yourself. Nothing of this world. A ghost. A haunting. A woman. A small, desperate, busy woman, here and not here, back and forth, out of her time, back from the grave, ill-omened, bringing grief and ruin: a message that nothing is what it seems, that God is dead and the forces of evil abroad and unstoppable. Does Angel hear, or not hear?

Angel through her fear, wants to go to the bathroom. She is three months pregnant. Her bladder is weak. It wakes her in the night, crying out its need, and Angel, obeying, will slip cautiously out of bed, trying not to wake Edward. Edward needs unbroken sleep if he is to paint well the next day. Edward, even at the best of times, suspects that Angel tossing and turning, and moaning in her sleep, as she will, wakes him on purpose to annoy.

Angel has not yet told Edward that she is pregnant. She keeps putting it off. She has no real reason to believe he does not want babies: but he has not said he does want them, and to assume that Edward wants what other people want is dangerous.

Angel moans aloud: afraid to move, afraid not to move, afraid to hear, afraid not to hear. So the child Angel lay awake in her little white bed, listening to her mother moaning, afraid to move, afraid not to move, to hear or not to hear. Angel's mother was a shoe-shop girl who married the new assistant manager after a six-week courtship. That

135

her husband went on to make a fortune, writing thrillers that sold by the million, was both Dora's good fortune and tragedy. She lived comfortably enough on alimony, after all, in a way she could never have expected, until dying by mistake from an overdose of sleeping pills. After that Angel was brought up by a succession of her father's mistresses and au-pairs. Her father Terry liked Edward, that was something, or at any rate he had been relieved at his appearance on the scene. He had feared an element of caution in Angel's soul: that she might end up married to a solicitor or stockbroker. And artists were at least creative, and an artist such as Edward Holst might well end up rich and famous. Terry had six Holst canvases on his walls to hasten the process. Two were of his daughter, nude, thigh slackly falling away from her stubby fair bush. Angel, defeated – as her mother had been defeated. 'I love you, Dora, but you must understand. I am not *in* love with you.' As I'm in love with Helen, Audrey, Rita, whoever it was: off to meetings, parties, off on his literary travels, looking for fresh copy and new backgrounds, encountering always someone more exciting, more interesting, than an ageing ex shoe-shop assistant. Why couldn't Dora understand? Unreasonable of her to suffer, clutching the wretched Angel to her alarmingly slack bosom. Could he, Terry, really be the only animation of her flesh? There was a sickness in her love, clearly; unaccompanied as it was by the beauty which lends grace to importunity.

Angel had her mother's large, sad eyes. The reproach in them was in-built. Better Dora's heart had stopped (she'd thought it would: six months pregnant, she found Terry in the house-maid's bed. She, Dora, mistress of servants! What bliss!) and the embryo Angel never emerged to the light of day.

The noise above Angel stops. Ghosts! What nonsense! A fallen lath grating and rattling in the wind. What else? Angel regains her courage, slips her hand out from beneath Edward's thigh preparatory to leaving the bed for the bathroom. She will turn on all the lights and run. Edward wakes; sits up.

'What's that? What in God's name's that?'
'I can't hear anything,' says Angel, all innocence. Nor can she, not now. Edward's displeasure to contend with now; worse than the universe rattling its chains.
'Footsteps, in the attic. Are you deaf? Why didn't you wake me?'
'I thought I imagined it.'

But she can hear them, once again, as if with his ears. The same pattern across the floor and back. Footsteps or heartbeats. Quicker and quicker now, hastening with the terror and tension of escape.

Edward, unimaginably brave, puts on his slippers, grabs a broken banister (five of these on the landing – one day soon, some day, he'll get round to mending them – he doesn't want some builder, paid by Angel, bungling the job) and goes on up to the attic. Angel follows behind. He will not let her cower in bed. Her bladder aches. She says nothing about that. How can she? Not yet. Not quite yet. Soon. 'Edward, I'm pregnant.' She can't believe it's true, herself. She feels a child, not a woman.

'Is there someone there?'

Edward's voice echoes through the three dark attic rooms.

Silence. He gropes for and switches on the light. Empty, derelict rooms: plaster falling, laths hanging, wallpaper peeling. Floorboards broken. A few cans of paint, a pile of wallpaper rolls, old newspapers. Nothing else.

'It could have been mice,' says Edward, doubtfully.

'Can't you hear it?' asks Angel, terrified. The sound echoes in her ears: footsteps clattering over a pounding heart. But Edward can't, not any more.

'Don't start playing games,' he murmurs, turning back to warmth and bed. Angel scuttles down before him, into the bathroom; the noise in her head fades. A few drops of urine tinkle into the bowl.

Edward lies awake in bed: Angel can feel his wakefulness, his increasing hostility towards her, before she is so much as back in the bedroom.

'Your bladder's very weak. Angel,' he complains. 'Something else you inherited from your mother?'

Something else, along with what? Suicidal tendencies, alcoholism, a drooping bosom, a capacity for being betrayed, deserted and forgotten?

Not forgotten by me, Mother. I don't forget. I love you. Even when my body cries out beneath the embraces of this man, this lover, this husband, and my mouth forms words of love, promises of eternity, still I don't forget. I love you, Mother.

138

'I don't know about my mother's bladder,' murmurs Angel rashly.

'Now you're going to keep me awake all night,' says Edward. 'I can feel it coming. You know I've nearly finished a picture.'
'I'm not going to say a word,' she says, and then, fulfilling his prophecy, sees fit to add, 'I'm pregnant.'

Silence. Stillness. Sleep?

No, a slap across nostrils, eyes, mouth. Edward has never hit Angel before. It is not a hard slap: it contains the elements of a caress.

'Don't even joke about it,' says Edward, softly.

'But I am pregnant.'

Silence. He believes her. Her voice made doubt impossible.

'How far?' Edward seldom asks for information. It is an act which infers ignorance, and Edward likes to know more than anyone else in the entire world.

'Three and a half months.'

He repeats the words, incredulous.

'Too far gone to do anything,' says Angel, knowing now why she did not tell Edward earlier, and the knowledge making her voice cold and hard. Too far gone for the abortion he will most certainly want her to have. So much for the fruits of love. Love? What's love? Sex, ah, that's another thing. Love has babies: sex has abortions.

But Angel will turn sex into love – yes, she will – seizing it by the neck, throttling it till it gives up and takes the weaker path. Love! Edward is right to be frightened, right to hate her.

'I hate you,' he says, and means it. 'You mean to destroy me.'

'I'll make sure it doesn't disturb your nights,' says Angel, Angel of the bristly fair bush, 'if that's what you're worrying about. And you won't have to support it. I do that, anyway. Or my father does.'

Well, how dare she! Angel, not nearly as nice as she thought. Soft-eyed, vicious Angel.

Slap, comes the hand again, harder. Angel screams, he shouts; she collapses, crawls about the floor – he spurns her, she begs forgiveness; he spits his hatred, fear, and she her misery. If the noise above continues, certainly no one hears it, there is so much going on below. The rustlings of the night erupting into madness. Angel is suddenly quiet, whimpering, lying on the floor; she squirms. At first Edward thinks she is acting, but her white lips and taloned fingers convince him that something is wrong with her body and not just her mind. He gets her back on the bed and rings the doctor. Within an hour Angel finds herself in a hospital with a suspected ectopic pregnancy. They delay the operation and the pain subsides; just one of those things, they shrug. Edward has to interrupt his painting the next afternoon to collect her from the hospital.

'What was it? Hysteria?' he enquires.

'I dare say!'

'Well, you had a bad beginning, what with your mother and all,' he concedes, kissing her nose, nibbling her earlobe. It is forgiveness; but Angel's eyes remain unusually cold. She stays in bed, after Edward has left it and gone back to his studio, although the floors remain unswept and the dishes unwashed.

Angel does not say what is in her mind, what she knows to be true. That he is disappointed to see both her and the baby back, safe and sound. He had hoped the baby would die, or failing that, the mother would die and the baby with her. He is pretending forgiveness, while he works out what to do next.

In the evening the doctor comes to see Angel. He is a slight man with a sad face: his eyes, she thinks, are kind behind his pebble glasses. His voice is slow and gentle. I expect his wife is happy, thinks Angel, and actually envies her. Some middle-aged, dowdy, provincial doctor's wife, envied by Angel! Rich, sweet, young and pretty Angel. The efficient secretary, lovable barmaid, and now the famous artist's wife! Once, for two rash weeks, even an art school model.

The doctor examines her, then discreetly pulls down her nightie to cover her breasts and moves the sheet up to cover her crotch. If he were my father, thinks Angel, he would not hang my naked portrait on his wall for the entertainment of his friends. Angel had not known until this moment that she minded.

'Everything's doing nicely inside there,' says the doctor. 'Sorry to rush you off like that, but we can't take chances.'

Ah, to be looked after. Love. That's love. The doctor shows no inclination to go.

'Perhaps I should have a word with your husband,' he suggests. He stands at the window gazing over daffodils and green fields. 'Or is he very busy?'

'He's painting,' says Angel. 'Better not disturb him now. He's had so many interruptions lately, poor man.'
'I read about him in the Sunday supplement,' says the doctor.
'Well, don't tell him so. He thought it vulgarised his work.'

'Did you think that?'

Me? Does what I think have anything to do with anything?

'I thought it was quite perceptive, actually,' says Angel, and feels a surge of good humour. She sits up in bed.

'Lie down,' he says. 'Take things easy. This is a large house. Do you have any help? Can't afford it?'
'It's not that. It's just why should I expect some other woman to do my dirty work?'

'Because she might like doing it and you're pregnant, and if you can afford it, why not?'

'Because Edward doesn't like strangers in the house. And what else have I got to do with my life? I might as well clean as anything else.'

'It's isolated out here,' he goes on. 'Do you drive?'

'Edward needs peace to paint,' says Angel. 'I do drive but Edward has a thing about women drivers.'

'You don't miss your friends?'

'After you're married,' says Angel, 'you seem to lose contact. It's the same for everyone, isn't it?'

'Um,' says the doctor. And then, 'I haven't been in this house for fifteen years. It's in a better state now than it was then. The house was divided into flats, in those days. I used to visit a nice young woman who had the attic floor. Just above this. Four children, and the roof leaked; a husband who spent his time drinking cider in the local pub and only came home to beat her.'

'Why did she stay?'

'How can such women leave? How do they afford it? Where do they go? What happens to the children?' His voice is sad.

'I suppose it's money that makes the difference. With money, a woman's free,' says Angel, trying to believe it.

'Of course,' says the doctor. 'But she loved her husband. She couldn't bring herself to see him for what he was. Well, it's hard. For a certain kind of woman, at any rate.'

Hard, indeed, if he has your soul in his safe-keeping, to

143

be left behind at the bar, in the pub, or in some other woman's bed, or in a seat in the train on his literary travels. Careless!

'But it's not like that for you, is it?' says the doctor calmly. 'You have money of your own, after all.'

Now how does he know that? Of course, the Sunday supplement article.

'No one will read it,' wept Angel, when Edward looked up, stony-faced from his first perusal of the fashionable columns. 'No one will notice. It's tucked away at the very bottom.'

So it was. 'Edward's angelic wife Angel, daughter of best-selling crime writer Terry Toms, has smoothed the path upwards, not just with the soft smiles our cameraman has recorded, but by enabling the emergent genius to forswear the cramped and inconvenient, if traditional, artist's garret for a sixteenth-century farmhouse in greenest Gloucestershire. It is interesting, moreover, to ponder whether a poor man would have been able to develop the white-on-white techniques which have made Holst's work so noticeable: or whether the sheer price of paint these days would not have deterred him.'

'Edward, I didn't say a word to that reporter, not a word,' she said, when the ice showed signs of cracking, days later.
'What are you talking about?' he asked, turning slow, unfriendly eyes upon her.
'The article. I know it's upset you. But it wasn't my fault.'

144

'Why should a vulgar article in a vulgar newspaper upset me?'

And the ice formed over again, thicker than ever. But he went to London for two days, presumably to arrange his next show, and on his return casually mentioned that he'd seen Ray while he was there.

Angel had cleaned, baked, and sewed curtains in his absence, hoping to soften his heart towards her on his return: and lay awake all the night he was away, the fear of his infidelity so agonising as to make her contemplate suicide, if only to put an end to it. She could not ask for reassurance. He would throw the fears so neatly back at her. 'Why do you think I should want to sleep with anyone else? Why are you so guilty? Because that's what you'd do if you were away from me?'

Ask for bread and be given stones. Learn self-sufficiency: never show need. Little, tough Angel of the soft smiles, hearing some other woman's footsteps in the night, crying for another's grief. Well, who wants a soul, tossed here and there by teasing hands, over-bruised and over-handled. Do without it!

Edward came home from London in a worse mood than he'd left, shook his head in wondering stupefaction at his wife's baking – 'I thought you said we were cutting down on carbo-hydrates' – and shut himself into his studio for twelve hours, emerging just once to say – 'Only a mad woman would hang curtains in an artist's studio, or else a silly rich girl playing at artist's wife, and in public at that' – and thrusting the new curtains back into her arms, vanished inside again.

Angel felt that her mind was slowing up, and puzzled over the last remark for some time before realising that Edward was still harking back to the Sunday supplement article.

'I'll give away the money if you like,' she pleaded through the keyhole. 'If you'd rather. And if you want not to be married to me I don't mind.' That was before she was pregnant.

Silence.

Then Edward emerged laughing, telling her not to be so ridiculous, bearing her off to bed, and the good times were restored. Angel sang about the house, forgot her pill, and got pregnant.

'You have money of your own, after all,' says the doctor. 'You're perfectly free to come and go.'
'I'm pregnant,' says Angel. 'The baby has to have a father.'
'And your husband's happy about the baby?'
'Oh yes!' says Angel. 'Isn't it a wonderful day!'

And indeed today the daffodils nod brightly under a clear sky. So far, since first they budded and bloomed, they have been obliged to droop beneath the weight of rain and mist. A disappointing spring. Angel had hoped to see the countryside leap into energy and colour, but life returned only slowly, it seemed, struggling to surmount the damage of the past: cold winds and hard frosts, unseasonably late. 'Or at any rate,' adds Angel, softly, unheard, as the doctor goes, 'he *will* be happy about the baby.'

Angel hears no more noises in the night for a week or so.

There had been misery in the attic rooms, and the misery had ceased. Good times can wipe out bad. Surely!

Edward sleeps soundly and serenely: she creeps from bed to bathroom without waking him. He is kind to her and even talkative, on any subject, that is, except that of her pregnancy. If it were not for the doctor and her stay in the hospital, she might almost think she was imagining the whole thing. Edward complains that Angel is getting fat, as if he could imagine no other cause for it but greed. She wants to talk to someone about hospitals, confinements, layettes, names – but to whom?

She tells her father on the telephone – 'I'm pregnant.'

'What does Edward say?' asks Terry, cautiously.

'Nothing much,' admits Angel.

'I don't suppose he does.'

'There's no reason *not* to have a baby,' ventures Angel.

'I expect he rather likes to be the centre of attention.' It is the nearest Terry has ever got to a criticism of Edward.

Angel laughs. She is beyond believing that Edward could ever be jealous of her, ever be dependent upon her.

'Nice to hear you happy, at any rate,' says her father wistfully. His twenty-year-old girlfriend has become engaged to a salesman of agricultural machinery, and although she has offered to continue the relationship the other side of

147

marriage, Terry feels debased and used, and was obliged to break off the liaison. He has come to regard his daughter's marriage to Edward in a romantic light. The young bohemians!

'My daughter was an art school model before she married Edward Holst . . . you've heard of him? It's a real Rembrandt and Saskia affair.' He even thinks lovingly of Dora: if only she'd understood, waited for youth to wear itself out. Now he's feeling old and perfectly capable of being faithful to an ex shoe-shop assistant. If only she weren't dead and gone!

An art school model. Those two weeks! Why had she done it? What devil wound up her works and set poor Angel walking in the wrong direction? It was in her nature, surely, as it was in her mother's to follow the paths to righteousness, fully clothed.

Nightly, Edward studied her naked body, kissing her here, kissing her there, parting her legs. Well, marriage! But now I'm pregnant, now I'm pregnant. Oh, be careful. That hard lump where my soft belly used to be. Be careful! Silence, Angel. Don't speak of it. It will be the worse for you and your baby if you do.

Angel knows it.

Now Angel hears the sound of lovemaking up in the empty attic, as she might hear it in hotels in foreign lands. The couplings of strangers in an unknown tongue – only the cries and breathings universal, recognisable anywhere.

The sounds chill her: they do not excite her. She thinks of

148

the mother of four who lived in this house with her drunken, violent husband. Was that what kept you by his side? The chains of fleshly desire? Was it the thought of the night that got you through the perils of the day?

What indignity, if it were so.

Oh, I imagine it. I, Angel, half-mad in my unacknowledged pregnancy, my mind feverish, and the doctor's anecdotes feeding the fever – I imagine it! I must!

Edward wakes.

'What's that noise?'
'What noise?'
'Upstairs.'
'I don't hear anything.'
'You're deaf.'
'What sort of noise?'

But Edward sleeps again. The noise fades, dimly. Angel hears the sound of children's voices. Let it be a girl, dear Lord, let it be a girl.

'Why do you want a girl?' asks the doctor, on Angel's fourth monthly visit to the clinic.

'I'd love to dress a girl,' says Angel vaguely, but what she means is, if it's a girl, Edward will not be so – what is the word? – hardly jealous, difficult perhaps. Dreadful. Yes, dreadful.

Bright-eyed Edward: he walks with Angel now – long walks

up and over stiles, jumping streams, leaping stones. Young Edward. She has begun to feel rather old, herself.

'I am a bit tired,' she says, as they set off one night for their moonlit walk.

He stops, puzzled.

'Why are you tired?'
'Because I'm pregnant,' she says, in spite of herself.
'Don't start that again,' he says, as if it were hysteria on her part. Perhaps it is.

That night, he opens her legs so wide she thinks she will burst. 'I love you,' he murmurs in her nibbled ear, 'Angel, I love you. I do love you.' Angel feels the familiar surge of response, the holy gratitude, the willingness to die, to be torn apart if that's what's required. And then it stops. It's gone. Evaporated! And in its place, a new strength. A chilly icicle of non-response, wonderful, cheerful. No. It isn't right; it isn't what's required: on the contrary. 'I love you,' she says in return, as usual; but crossing her fingers in her mind, forgiveness for a lie. Please God, dear God, save me, help me save my baby. It is not me he loves, but my baby he hates: not me he delights in, but the pain he causes me, and knows he does. He does not wish to take root in me: all he wants to do is root my baby out. I don't love him. I never have. It is sickness. I must get well. Quickly.

'Not like that,' says Angel, struggling free – bold, unkind, prudish Angel – rescuing her legs. 'I'm pregnant. I'm sorry, but I am pregnant.'

Edward rolls off her, withdraws.

'Christ, you can be a monster. A real ball-breaker.'

'Where are you going?' asks Angel, calm and curious.
Edward is dressing. Clean shirt; cologne. Cologne!

'To London.'
'Why?'
'Where I'm appreciated.'
'Don't leave me alone. Please.' But she doesn't mean it.
'Why not?'
'I'm frightened. Here alone at night.'
'Nothing ever frightened you.' Perhaps he is right.

Off he goes; the car breaking open the silence of the night.
It closes again. Angel is alone.

Tap, tap, tap, up above. Starting up as if on signal. Back and
forward. To the attic bed which used to be, to the wardrobe
which once was; the scuffle of the suitcase on the floor. Goodbye. I'm going. I'm frightened here. The house is haunted.
Someone upstairs, downstairs. Oh, women everywhere, don't
think your misery doesn't seep into walls, creep downstairs,
and then upstairs again. Don't think it will ever be done
with, or that the good times wipe it out. They don't.

Angel feels her heart stop and start again. A neurotic
symptom, her father's doctor had once said. It will get better,
he said, when she's married and has babies. Everything gets
better for women when they're married with babies. It's
their natural state. Angel's heart stops all the same, and
starts again, for good or bad.

151

Angel gets out of bed, slips on her mules with their sharp little heels and goes up the attic stairs. Where does she find the courage? The light, reflected up from the hallway, is dim. The noise from the attic stops. Angel hears only — what? — the rustling noise of old newspapers in a fresh wind. That stops, too. As if a film were now running without sound. And coming down towards Angel, a small, tired woman in a nightie, slippers silent on the stairs, stopping to stare at Angel as Angel stares at her. Her face marked by bruises.

'How can I see that,' wonders Angel, now unafraid, 'since there isn't any light?'

She flicks on the switch, hand trembling, and in the light, as she'd known, there is nothing to be seen except the empty stairs and the unmarked dust upon them.

Angel goes back to the bedroom and sits on the bed.

'I saw a ghost,' she tells herself, calmly enough. Then fear reasserts itself: panic at the way the universe plays tricks. Quick, quick! Angel pulls her suitcase out from under the bed — there are still traces of wedding confetti within — and tap-tap she goes, with sharp little footsteps, from the wardrobe to the bed, from the chest of drawers and back again, not so much packing as retrieving, salvaging. Something out of nothing!

Angel and her predecessor, rescuing each other, since each was incapable of rescuing herself, and rescue always comes, somehow. Or else death.

Tap, tap, back and forth, into the suitcase, out of the house.

The garden gate swings behind her.

Angel, bearing love to a safer place.

Spirit of the House

Some time after the trouble with Jenny began, Christine wrote off to a professor of psychical research who lived in California. 'Whenever Jenny comes into the room,' Christine wrote, 'I feel cold. So I know there's *something* wrong with her. But what exactly it is?' She had an answer sooner than she expected. The professor wrote that the presence of evil was often registered, by sensitives, in this manner; and was there a bad smell as well?

Now Jenny did indeed quite often smell strongly of carbolic but Christine felt that this was not in itself significant. The soap provided for employees up at the Big House was a job lot of hard, orange, carbolic tablets, bought cheap from an army surplus store, and Jenny washed herself with it, lavishly and often. Christine always took Mornay's Lavender to work with her, the more sweetly to wash her pretty hands. Christine liked to smell nice, and her husband Luke liked her to smell nice, and how he could put up with Jenny smelling of carbolic, Christine could not understand. And how he could love her, Christine could understand still less.

But carbolic was not, in itself, a bad smell, and nothing like the stench of sulphur and decomposition associated with the presence of the Devil. Enough however, that the feeling of cold wafted around Jenny like an odour. She could be said to smell cold. Christine discontinued her correspondence with the Californian professor for fear of discovering worse. She prayed instead.

'Dear God, let him get over her. Dear God, let her not harm the baby. Dear God, let them believe me.'

But God seemed not to be listening. Luke went on loving Jenny, Jenny went on looking after Baby Emmy, and no one believed Christine when she said that Jenny was not to be trusted.

Christine had been married to Luke for nineteen years. She loved her husband with an energetic and consuming passion, well able to withstand his occasional adoration of passing girls. She would treat him, when he was thus enamoured, with a fond indulgence, saying, 'Well, men are like that, aren't they?' and waiting for common sense and reason to return, and uxorious content to shine once again from his gentle eyes. But Jenny was dangerous – Christine had suspected something unwholesome about her from the very first. In retrospect it was hard to tell, of course, quite when she had begun to think it – before Luke started mooning after Jenny, or after. But surely it was before – a sickly, chilly menace, a sudden shiver down the spine? Evil, the professor had written. Or perhaps he only wrote that, knowing what she wanted to hear? Americans were strange.

Even so, the damage was done. Now Christine feared for Luke, body and soul, and feared for Emmy, Lord Mader's baby daughter, even more. Jenny was Emmy's nanny. Little, pretty, safe words, adding up to something monstrous.

And of course if Christine murmured against Jenny, the other members of the staff assumed that Christine was jealous, and discredited what she said. Christine's husband, everyone knew, was in love with Jenny, trailing after her, gazing after her.

'But look,' Christine felt like saying, 'he's been in love a dozen times in as many years. It's just the way he is. I don't mind. He's a genius, you see. A mathematical genius, not one of your artistic geniuses, but a genius all the same. My feeling about Jenny is nothing to do with Luke's feeling for her.'

But the rest of the staff were dull, if good-hearted, and had their preconceptions about the world, which nothing now would shake: it was almost as if the chilly presence of Jenny had cemented in these preconceptions. Their vision narrowed to what they already knew. Christine concluded that Jenny had a strange deadening power over everyone, excepting only, for some reason, herself.

Jenny had a white, dead face and large, pale eyes she magnified with round owl spectacles, and short plain hair and a child's body. The face was thirty, the body was thirteen. Perhaps that was her power – the desire of the grown man for the prepubertal girl? A sickly and insidious love! And did the women perhaps remember themselves at thirteen and set Jenny free now, to do what they would have liked then?

Christine herself, at forty, was plump and maternal and pretty and busy. There could be nothing unhealthy in anyone's desire for her, and many did desire her, but she seldom noticed. She loved Luke.

Christine, the Doris Day of Mader House! Wonderful Mader House, Stately Home, giving the lucky villagers of Maderley full employment! With its Elizabethan chimneys, and Jacobean mullions, Georgian casements and Victorian tiles, it still remained imposing, if hardly gracious. Its lands and gardens, its ancient oaks, its Disneyland and zoo, its Sunday lunches with Lord and Lady Mader (fifty pounds a place-setting), made it popular with the millions. Lord Mader was often indisposed at these luncheons and his young brother Martin sent in his place, but the third Lady Mader, Mara, was always there. She was young and did as she was told, as did the villagers.

The Maders, their disparagers murmured, once a powerful and wealthy family, were now a handful of publicity-seeking degenerates. Even Christine, who loved to be loyal, increasingly saw truth in this observation. Yves, the present Lord, was thrice married. His first wife had been barren, and for that reason divorced. Lucien, son by his second wife, was a junkie, and Lucien's little sister Deborah now played the lead in skin flicks. Yet these seemed matters of mirth rather than shame to Yves. A further son, Piers, was in real estate, and considered too boring for discussion. Left a widower by his second wife's suicide, Yves had promptly married Mara, a twenty-year-old Greek heiress, and sired little Emmy.

Yves had selected Jenny from over two hundred applicants

for the post of Nanny. He prided himself on being a good judge of character.

'Does he love the baby?' people would ask Christine. 'Oh yes,' she'd reply, adding in her heart, 'as much as he loves anything, which isn't very much.' The pressure of the words grew and grew and she was frightened that one day she would say them aloud.
'And the mother?'
'She's not very much at home, but I'm sure she does.' Christine was nice. She wanted to think well of everyone.

Mara loved treats and outings and hunting, and occasions on which she could wear a tiara, and the Mader family jewels – or, rather, their replicas. The originals had been sold in the thirties; and Maderley House itself would have followed in the fifties, had not Yves discovered that the people's fascination with their aristocracy could be turned to excellent financial account; whereupon he flung open the gates, and filled up the moat, and turned the stables into restaurants, and himself into a public show.

The show business side of Maderley was in Christine's charge – it was she who organised the guides, the cleaners, the caterers, even the vets for sick animals. She saw to brochures, catalogues and souvenirs. She took the takings to the bank. She had the status in the household of someone dedicated, who is despised for their dedication. She was underpaid, and mocked for being so by those who underpaid her, and did not notice.

Christine's husband Luke sat in the Great Library and worked out efficient mathematical formulae for the winning of the pools. Yves had once met, over dinner, a Nobel Prize winner, a mathematician, who had convinced him of the practicality of working out such formulae, computer-aided. Yves promptly had a computer-terminal installed in the Great Library, and Luke installed likewise. Visitors gawped at both between two and three on Wednesdays. Luke had a first-class honours degree in mathematics from Oxford. He had been a Maderley child with a peculiar gift for numbers and few social skills. He had returned to the village, married to Christine, a girl from far away, to write textbooks for graduates, which he did slowly, with difficulty, and for very little money.

The Great Library! There Christine fed the computer with data about visitors, gate takings, capital costs and so forth. And here Luke puzzled over his formulae, and here Jenny liked to sit in the winter sun beneath the mullioned windows, and rock the baby's pram, and watch Luke at work. The baby never cried. Sometimes it whimpered. The cover was pulled up well over its face.

Christine had tried to say something to Yves about Jenny and the baby.

'Yves' – his employees were instructed to call him by his Christian name – 'can I talk to you about Jenny?'
'What do you want to say?' He was unfriendly. She knew he did not like trouble. It was her function, after all, to keep it away from him. She had once asked for a rise in her wages, and the same shuttered, cold look had fallen across his face, as it now did, when she wanted to talk about Jenny. 'I don't think she's very good with the baby,' said Christine, tentatively, and wanted to go on and say, 'My

159

Lord, I have seen bruises on the baby's arm. I don't like the way the baby whimpers instead of crying. I don't like the thinness of the baby's wrists. A baby's wrists should be chubby and creased, not bony.' But she didn't speak. She hesitated, looking at his cold face, and was lost.

'You mean she's too good with your husband, Christine,' was all Yves said. 'You sort out your own problems, don't come running to me.'

Christine, later that day, came across Yves with Jenny. They were together in the library. He had his hands on her thin shoulders: he, who seldom touched anyone. What were they saying?

Christine heard the baby make its little mewling cry, but Yves did not even glance into the pram.

Christine said to Mrs Scott the housekeeper, 'I'm worried about that baby. I don't think she gets enough to eat.'
Mrs Scott said, 'You don't know anything about babies. You've never had one. Jenny's a trained Norland nanny. She knows what she's doing.'

Jenny sat next to Mrs Scott at the staff lunch that day. They seemed very companionable.

Christine watched Luke watching Jenny being companionable with Mrs Scott, and the staff watched Christine watching Luke watching Jenny, and sniggered.

Christine telephoned the Norland nanny organisation, and they had no record of a Jenny Whitstone on their books.

Christine watched Jenny hold the baby's bottle an inch or so from the baby's mouth, so that the baby stopped whimpering and rooted with its mouth towards the warm, sweet smell and found it, and Christine watched Jenny tug out the bottle after the first few mouthfuls and put it back on the shelf. The baby moaned.

'What did you do that for?' asked Christine.

'I don't want the baby getting too fat,' said Jenny. 'It's a terrible thing to be fat.'

And Jenny eyed Christine's plump form with cold distaste.

Luke stopped making love to Christine altogether.

'It wouldn't be fair to you,' said Luke. 'How can I make love to you when I'm thinking of her? I wish I could, but I can't.'

'Why, why do you love her?' begged Christine.

But he didn't know, couldn't say.

It seemed to Christine that Luke felt cold in bed, as if his flesh was dying.

She spoke to the guides about Jenny, at their Monday morning meeting, where such things were discussed as meal breaks and the positioning of the silken ropes which guarded certain rooms and passages from the touch and view of ordinary people. 'Where did she come from?' Christine asked. 'Does anyone know?'

No one seemed to. It was as if she had always been there, along with the house itself, along with the family: the worm, or whatever it was, that nibbled away at the souls of the rich, so that born angels, they grew up devils.

For what could become of them but this? Generation succeeding generation: heartless mothers, distant fathers, and the distress of this made light of, by a surfeit of manners and money?

'The scale's all wrong,' Christine said in her heart. 'The house is just too big for people.'

Life's battles, life's events, triumphs and disasters – all were rendered puny by the lofty ceilings. Words of love and grief alike, hate and joy, all were muted beneath the arching vaults of the great hall, were sopped up and made one by ancient panelling. The stair was too high for the child to climb, or the old woman to descend. Marriages were lost in a bed so big it made passion trivial: the sexual act ridiculous under the cold eyes of ceiling cherubs. And animals! The love of dumb beasts put before the love of people; the death of a horse marking the year more than the death of a child; kennels always warmer than the nurseries. Manners replacing morals.

'They're born like anyone else,' Christine said in her heart, never aloud. 'And then I don't know what happens, but they end up monsters.'

So, now, it seemed to Christine, the damage which little Emmy could expect in the course of the next twenty years was being, at the hands of Jenny, inflicted upon her in as many months.

'I know why you love her,' she said presently to Luke, 'it's because she's the spirit of the House. And it's sickening and disgusting, and everyone loves it. Except me.'

'That isn't why I love her,' said Luke. 'And if you feel like that about the House, why go on working here?'

'What else could I do round here? There's no employment except at Maderley.'

But in spite of what she said, she stayed and she knew she stayed because she too, like Luke, was still under the spell of the Big House, and felt honoured by the company of Yves, whom she was privileged to call by his Christian name, and because she did not want to leave Emmy and Luke to the mercies of Jenny.

Lady Mara was due back from the Bahamas. The whole house gleamed with polish and glowed with flowers.

But Emmy was listless, and blinked a good deal, and flinched and grizzled the day Lady Mara came back.

'She isn't very pretty,' said Mara, disappointed, peering into the pram, and after that seldom asked to see the child at all. She rode to hounds a good deal, along with farmers and carpet manufacturers.

'I wish you wouldn't,' complained Yves. 'Only the bourgeoisie go hunting these days.' But Mara was regaining her spirit, and learning how to do not what she was told, and she persisted, slashing at grasses with her riding crop, as if she'd like to slash at life itself.

Presently, Christine came across Jenny in the Great Library. Jenny had taken Emmy, for once, out of her pram. Jenny stood there, among ten thousand books, which were beautifully bound but never read, turning her owl eyes up to where the sunlight glanced through the windows, so that her spectacles dazzled, and seemed to retain the blinding shine even when she turned her head out of the sunlight to face Christine. Jenny, with her child's thighs in their tight, faded jeans, and budding breasts beneath a white T-shirt, and a dazzle where her face should be.

Jenny, with her soft, flat, slightly nasal voice, which could turn sharp and cruel and hard. Christine had often heard it. 'Christ, you little monster!' And slap, slap, thump, and then the weary grizzle again from Emmy.

Christine had never managed to get pregnant.
'Well,' the doctor had said, 'I dare say you have a child already, in your husband.'

Christine, cooking, nurturing, caring, worrying, had agreed with the doctor and not minded too much about their lack of children. Christine, after all, was the breadwinner. Perhaps what Luke saw in Jenny, suggested Christine, trying again, was his own unborn daughter? An incestuous love, given permission to live and thrive.

It was Yves who had given permission. Yes, he had. 'We all love Jenny,' Yves had said. 'Jenny saves us from our children.' Everyone except Christine, everyone's look said, watching Christine watching Luke watching Jenny, everyone loves Jenny.

Christine tried Yves' younger brother Martin, born by Caesarean while his mother lay dying from an overdose of sleeping pills and whisky, self-inflicted. Martin was the estate manager at Maderley. When Yves spoke to Martin it was in the same way he spoke to the upper servants – with a derisive politeness. Martin stuttered, so that Christine's conversation with him took a long time, and she was busy, needed at the tollgate with new parking tickets.

'Sir, I don't think Jenny is what she says. She isn't a Norland nurse at all. I checked up.'

'No one round here is what they claim to be,' said Martin, sadly. 'And the baby is Lady Mara's business, not ours.'

'Couldn't you say something to Yves?'

'Not really,' said Martin. 'If you feel strongly about it, say something yourself.'

'I have, but he just got angry and wouldn't listen.'

'The baby looks like any other baby to me,' said Martin. 'Not that I know much about them, of course.' One of Martin's eyes turned inwards – a squint which had been left untreated in infancy, and so remained.

'Yves is a very good judge of character,' said Martin. 'If he employed Jenny she must be all right.'

The next day Christine saw Jenny wheeling the baby in the grounds, and Martin was with her. Even Martin! Martin, saying goodbye to Jenny, pecked her on the cheek, and she turned her face so that once again her glasses glinted and dazzled and the space beneath the pram hood seemed black, like the mouth of hell.

When Jenny wheeled the baby into the kitchen that day Christine bent to pick the baby up.

'Don't pick up the baby,' said Jenny sharply. 'She's sleeping quietly.' But to Christine the baby looked not so much asleep, as dead. And then an eyelash fluttered against the

165

white cheek and Christine knew she was wrong. She went on counting sandwiches – two hundred ham, one hundred cheese – for the special Maderley tea, four pounds a head, served in the converted stable block.

'But *how* do you love her, *why* do you love her?'

She knew that she was nagging: she couldn't help it. She kept Luke awake at night now, working away at the truth. It was only while he slept that his body grew cold, and the pain of his answers was preferable to the chilly numbness of his sleep; she knew that, sleeping, he drifted off somewhere away from her, over the safe, surrounding walls of her love and, moth-like, floated towards the chilly, blinding light which used Jenny as its beacon.

It was at that time that she wrote to the professor of psychical research, and had confirmation of her fears. Jenny was evil.

'Lady Mara?'
'What is it, Christine?'

Lady Mara, broken arm in a sling – her horse had lurched and reared at nothing in particular, a sudden bright light in the grounds was all she could think of – was lately very much the grande dame. She would have bathed in asses' milk if she could.
'Lady Mara, I'm worried about the baby.'
'The baby is nothing to do with you. You look after the visitors and let Jenny look after the baby.'

Lady Mara was only twenty-one. The same age as Yves'

daughter, the one who presented her body at rude, amazing angles for the benefit of the camera, a publisher and a million wistful men. But a title and wealth, and the assumption of power, of the right to tell other people what to do and what to say, add up to more than years. Mara stared coldly. Christine fumbled. Christine was impertinent. If she didn't stop meddling she might have to go. There were more than enough only too ready to take her place. Mara said nothing. There was no need to. Christine fell silent.

Yves and Mara went away to attend a wedding. Five thousand pounds, they had heard, were to be spent on flowers for the marquees alone. Who would miss a wedding like that?

Christine found her husband Luke weeping in the conservatory.
'What's the matter, Luke?'
But he was frozen into silence. Presently, he thawed, as if warmed by Christine's presence, her arm round his shaking shoulders, and spoke.
'I asked her. I plucked up courage and asked her. I said I wanted to sleep with her more than anything in the world.'
'And?' How cold the pit of the stomach, where words strike their message home.
'She laughed at me. She told me I was old and flabby. She said I was weak. She said I was a failure. Am I these things, Christine?'
'Of course not.'
'I love her more than ever.'

Christine went to see Jenny in her bedroom. 'You leave my husband alone,' said Christine, 'or I'll kill you.'

'Get him to leave me alone,' said Jenny, laughing, a cold, dead laugh. How could you kill what was already dead?

The baby murmured in its cot. Christine looked at little Emmy. Her eyes were black, and swollen. Christine lifted the baby out of its cot.
'You leave that baby alone,' snapped Jenny. 'You poor jealous frustrated barren old bitch.'

It was the cry of the world, but it was not true. Christine's spirit was warm, loving and fecund.

Christine unwrapped little Emmy from her soft blankets and found that her back was bruised and her right leg hung oddly. Christine cradled the baby carefully in her arms and ran down long, long corridors, hung with family portraits, and down the great staircase, and into the reception area, where the tickets were taken, and rang all the bells she could, and Martin came, and Luke and three of the guides and Mrs Scott the housekeeper, and a cleaner; and Jenny followed after but stopped halfway down the stairs, in a little patch where the sun shone in, so she glowed all over, the source and not the reflection of light.

'Look,' said Christine, showing what was in her arms. 'Look! See what she's done to the baby?'

'It was an accident,' called Jenny, in her soft, nasal voice. 'You're all my friends. You know I wouldn't do it on purpose.'

But the sun had shone in upon the wrong stair. She was just too far away, her voice just a little too faint. Jenny's words meant nothing to the cluster of people gazing at the baby, Lord Mader's baby, with its swollen eyes and its blue-black back.

'I'll get an ambulance,' said Christine.
'Think of the publicity,' said Martin, but he spoke without much conviction. 'Yves won't like it.'
'Perhaps we'd better telephone him and get permission,' said Mrs Scott.
'Let me take the baby,' called Jenny. 'It's me Emmy loves. You're all strangers to her. She'll get better if I hold her.'

And what Jenny said was true, but she couldn't make up her mind to lose the sun and step another stair down into the hall, and she faltered and was lost.

Martin rang Yves. Christine had his number: flicked through her efficient files and found it at once.

'Yves,' said Martin, stuttering his message out. 'You'd better come back here. The baby's got a bruise on its back. Christine thinks we should call an ambulance.'
'Christine would,' said Yves, sourly. 'Well, stop her. We'll be right back.'

But Christine called the ambulance all the same. They took the baby away and just as well, because Yves and Mara didn't return for three days.

Emmy had a fractured skull, two broken ribs, a broken thigh and a damaged kidney, but they patched her up quite well, and returned her after eight weeks looking quite pretty, so that her mother picked her up and murmured endearments and nuzzled into her baby neck, and fortunately Emmy smiled at that moment and didn't cry, which would have spoiled everything.

Christine lost her job, and Yves abandoned his hopes of breaking the Great Proletariat Pools Swindle and fired Luke too.

'You'd think they'd be grateful for my saving their baby,' said Christine. 'But the upper classes are just plain twisted.' 'The Greeks used to kill the bearer of bad news,' said Luke, 'so think yourself lucky.'

The sight of the damaged baby had made him fall out of love with Jenny, and now he slept warm at night, and Christine beside him. Jenny did not lose her job, but at least she was no longer allowed to look after the baby. Instead, she did what Christine had been doing, for twice the money and with the help of an assistant.

'What a great judge of character Yves is!' said Christine sourly. Everyone she asked, and ask she did, everyone, agreed with her. The Maders were degenerate and decadent. She could say the words aloud now, not just in her heart.

Later she heard that Jenny had taken another post as nanny to two little girls whose mother had died, and that Yves had written her an excellent reference.

'Your employees reflect back on you,' said Luke. 'That's what it is.'

Christine wondered whether to telephone the father of the

two little girls and warn him, but knew she would never be believed. And perhaps, who was to say, there was someone like her in every little pocket of the world? Someone to save while others destroyed, or looked away. Wherever Jenny went, there would be someone like Christine.

'I loved her because she was evil,' said Luke, at last, explaining. 'She anaesthetised my moral nerve endings and that at the time was wonderful. And you were right: she was the spirit of the house.'

Watching Me, Watching You

The ghost liked the stairs best, where people passed quickly and occasionally, holding their feelings in suspense between the closing of one door and the opening of another. Mostly, the ghost slept. He preferred sleep. But sometimes the sense of something important happening, some crystallisation of the past or omen for the future, would wake him, and he would slither off the stair and into one room or another of the house to see what was going on. Presently, he wore an easy path of transition into a particular room on the first floor – as sheep will wear an easy path in the turf by constant trotting to and fro. Here, as the seasons passed, a plane tree pressed closer and closer against the window, keeping out light and warmth. The various cats which lived out their lives in the house seldom went into this small damp back room, and seemed to feel the need to race up and down that portion of the stairs the ghost favoured, though sitting happily enough at the bottom of the stairs, or on the top landing.

Many houses contain ghosts. (It would be strange if they didn't.) Mostly they sleep, or wake so seldom their presence is not noticed, let alone minded. If a glass falls off a shelf in 1940, and a door opens by itself in 1963, and a sense of oppression is felt in 1971, and knocking sounds are heard on Christmas Day, 1980 – who wants to make anything of that? Four inexplicable happenings in a week call for exorcism – the same number spread over forty years call for nothing more than a shrug and a stiff drink.

66 Aldermans Drive, Bristol. The house had stood for a hundred and thirty years, and the ghost had slept and occasionally sighed and slithered sideways, and otherwise done little else but puff out a curtain on a still day for all but ten of those. He entered the house on the shoulders of a parlour maid. She had been to a seance in the hope of raising her dead lover, but had raised something altogether more elusive, if at least sleepier, instead. The maid had stayed in the house until she died, driving her mistress to suicide and marrying the master the while, and the ghost had stayed too, long after all were dead, and the house empty, with paper peeling off the walls, and the banisters broken, and carpets rotting on the floors, and dust and silence everywhere.

The ghost slept, and woke again to the sound of movement, and different voices. The new people were numerous: they warmed gnarled winter hands before gas fires, and the smell of boiled cabbage and sweat wafted up the stairs, and exhaustion and indifference prevailed. In the back room on the first floor, presently, a girl gave birth to a baby. The ghost sighed and puffed out the curtains. In this room, earlier, the maid's mistress had hanged herself, making a swinging shadow against the wall in the gaslight shining from the stairs. The ghost had a sense of justice, or at any rate balance. He slept again.

The house emptied. Rain came through broken tiles into the back room. A man with a probe came and pierced into the rotten beams of roof and floor, and shook his head and laughed. The tree thrust a branch through the window, and a sparrow flew in, and couldn't get out, and died, and after mice and insects and flies had finished with it, was nothing more than two slender white bones, placed crosswise.

It was 1965. The front door opened and a man and a woman entered, and such was their natures that the ghost was alert at once. The man's name was Maurice: he was burly and warm-skinned; his hands were thick and crude, labourer's hands, but clean and soft. His hair was pale and tightly curled; he was bearded; his eyes were large and heavily hooded. He looked at the house as if he were already its master: as if he cared nothing for its rotten beams and its leaking roof.

'We'll have it,' he said. She laughed. It was a nervous laugh, which she used when she was frightened. She had a small cross face half-lost in a mass of coarse red hair. She was tiny-waisted, big-bosomed and long-legged; her limbs lean and freckly. Her fingers were long and fragile. 'But it's falling down,' said Vanessa. 'How can we afford it?'
'Look at the detail on the cornices!' was all he said. 'I'm sure they're original.'
'I expect we can make something of it,' she said.

She loved him. She would do what she could for him. The ghost sensed cruelty, somewhere: he bustled around, stirring the air.

'It's very draughty,' she complained.

They looked into the small back room on the first floor and even he shivered.

'I'll never make anything of this room,' she said.

'Vanessa,' he said. 'I trust you to do something wonderful with everything.'

'Then I'll make it beautiful,' she said, loud and clear, marking out her future. 'Even this, for you.'

The plane tree rubbed against the window pane.

'It's just a question of lopping a branch or two,' he said.

One night, after dark, when builders' trestles were everywhere, and the sour smell of damp lime plaster was on the stairs, Maurice spread a blanket for Vanessa in the little back room.

'Not here,' she said.

'It's the only place that isn't dusty,' he said.

He made love to her, his broad, white body covering her narrow, freckled one altogether.

'Today the divorce came through,' he said.

Other passions split the air. The ghost felt them. Outside in the alley which ran behind the house, beneath the plane tree, stood another woman. Her face was round and sweet, her hair was short and mousy, her eyes bright, bitter and wet. In the house the girl cried out and the man groaned; and the watcher's face became empty, drained of sweetness, left expressionless, a vacuum into which something had to flow. The ghost left with her, on her shoulders.

'I have fibrositis now,' said Anne, 'as well as everything else.' She said it to herself, into the mirror, when she was back

175

home in the basement of the house in Upton Park, where once she and Maurice had lived and built their life. She had to say it to herself, because there was no one else to say it to, except their child Wendy, and Wendy was only four and lay asleep in a pile of blankets on the floor, her face and hands sticky and unwashed. Anne threw an ashtray at the mirror and cracked it, and Wendy woke and cried. 'Seven years' bad luck,' said Anne. 'Well, who's counting!'

Sweetness had run out: sourness took its place: she too had marked out her future.

The ghost found a space against the wall between the barred windows of the room, and took up residence there, and drowsed, waking sometimes to accompany Anne on her midnight vigils to 66 Aldermans Drive. Presently he wore an easy route for himself, slipping and slithering between the two places, and no longer needed her for the journey. Sometimes he was here, sometimes there.

In Aldermans Drive he found a painted stairwell and a mended banister, but stairs which were still uncarpeted, and a cat which howled and shot upstairs. The ghost moved in to the small back room and the door pushed open in his path and shadows swung and shifted against the wall.

Vanessa was wearing jeans. She and Maurice were papering the room with bright patterned paper. They were laughing: she had glue in her hair.
'When we're rich,' she was saying, 'I'll never do this kind of thing again. We'll always have professionals in to do it.'

176

'When we're rich!' He yearned for it.

'Of course we'll be rich. You'll write a bestseller; you're far better than anyone else. Genius will out!'

If he felt she misunderstood the nature of genius, or was insensitive to what he knew by instinct, that popularity and art are at odds, he said nothing. He indulged her. He kissed her. He loved her.

'What are those shadows on the wall?' she asked.

'We always get those in here,' he said. 'It's the tree against the window.'

'We'll have to get it lopped,' she said.

'It seems a pity,' he said. 'Such a wonderful old tree.'

He trimmed another length of paper.

'How can the tree be casting shadows?' she asked. 'The sun isn't out.'

'Some trick of reflected light,' said Maurice. The knife in his hand slipped, and he swore.

'It doesn't matter,' said Vanessa, looking at the torn paper, 'it doesn't have to be perfect. It's only Wendy's room. And then only for weekends. It's not as if she was going to be here all the time.'

'Perhaps you and I should have this room,' said Maurice, 'and Wendy could have the one next door. It overlooks the crescent. It has a view, and a balcony. She'll love it.'

'So would I,' said Vanessa.

'I don't want Wendy to feel second-best,' said Maurice. 'Not after all we've put her through.'

'All that's happened to her,' corrected Vanessa, tight lipped.

'And don't say "only Wendy",' he rebuked her. 'She is my child, after all.'

'It isn't fair! Why couldn't you be like other people? Why do you have to have a past?'

They worked in silence for a little, and the ghost writhed palely in the anger in the air, and then Vanessa relented and smiled and said, 'Don't let's quarrel,' and he said, 'You know I love you,' and the fine front room was Wendy's and the small back room was to house their marriage bed.

'I'm sure I closed the door,' said Vanessa presently, 'but now it's open.'

'The catch is weak,' said Maurice. 'I'll mend it when I can. There's just so much to do in a home this size,' and he sighed and the sigh exhaled out of the open window into the street.

'Goodbye,' said Vanessa.

'Why did you say goodbye?' asked Maurice.

'Because the net curtains flapped and whoever came in through the door was clearly going out by the window,' said Vanessa, thinking she was joking, too young and beautiful and far from death to mind an unseen visitor or so. The ghost whirled away on the remnant of Maurice's sigh, over the roof-tops and the brow of the hill, and down into Upton Park, where it was winter, no longer summer, and little Wendy was six, and getting out of bed, bare cold toes on chilly lino.

The ghost's observations were now from outside time. So a man might stand on a station overpass and watch a train go through beneath. Such a man could see, if he chose, any point along the train – in front of him the future, behind him the past, directly beneath him, changing always from past to future, his main rumbling, noisy perception of the present. The ghost keeps his gaze steadily forward.

The clock says five to nine; Anne is asleep in bed. Wendy shakes her awake.

'My feet are cold,' says the little girl.

'Then put on your slippers,' mourns the mother, out of sleep. It has been an uneasy, unsatisfying slumber. Once she lay next to Maurice and fancied she drew her strength out of his slumbering body, hot beside her, like some spiritual water bottle. She clings to the fancy in her mind: she refuses to sleep as she did when a child, composed and decent in solitude, providing her own warmth well enough.

'Won't I be late for school?' asks Wendy.

'No,' says Anne, in the face of all evidence to the contrary.

'It is ever so cold,' says Wendy. 'Can I light the gas fire?'

'No you can't,' says Anne. 'We can't afford it.'

'Daddy will pay the bill,' says Wendy, hopefully. But her mother just laughs.

'I'm frightened,' says Wendy, all else having failed. 'The curtains are waving about and the window isn't even open. Can I get into your bed?'

Anne moves over and the child gets in.

An egg teeters on the edge of the table, amidst the remnants of last night's chips and tomato sauce, and falls and smashes. Anne sits up in bed, startled into reaction.

'How did that happen?' she asks, aloud. But there is no one to reply, for Wendy has fallen asleep, and the ghost is spinning and spinning, nothing but a whirl of air in the corner of the eye, and no one listens to him, anyway.

Further forward still, and there's Vanessa, sitting up in bed, bouncy brown-nippled breasts half covered by fawn lace. It is a brass bed, finely filigreed. Maurice wears black silk pyjamas. He sits on the edge of the bed, while Vanessa sips fresh orange juice, and opens his letters.

'Any cheques?' asks Vanessa.

'Not today,' he says. Maurice is a writer. Cheques bounce through the letter box with erratic energy: bills come in with a calm, steady beat. It is a tortoise and hare situation, and the tortoise always wins.

'Perhaps you should change your profession,' she suggests. 'Be an engineer or go into advertising. I hate all this worry about money.'

A mirror slips upon its string on the wall, hangs sidewise. Neither notice.

'Is that a letter from Anne?' asks Vanessa. 'What does she want now?'

'It's her electricity bill,' he says.

'She's supposed to pay that out of her monthly cheque. She only sends you these demands to make you feel unhappy and guilty. She's jealous of us. How I despise jealousy! What a bitch she is!'

'She has a child to look after,' says Maurice. 'My child.'

'If I had your child, would you treat me better?' she asks.

'I treat you perfectly well,' he says, pulling the bedclothes back, rubbing black silk against beige lace, and the mirror falls off the wall altogether, startling them, stopping them.

'This whole room will have to be stripped out,' complains Vanessa. 'The plaster is rotten. I'll get arthritis from the damp.' Vanessa notices, sometimes, as she walks up and down the stairs, that her knees ache.

Wendy is ten. Anne's room has been painted white, and there are cushions on the chairs, and dirty washing is put in the basket, not left on the floor, and times are a little better. A little. There is passion in the air.

'Vanessa says I can stay all week not just weekends, and go to school from Aldermans Drive!' says Wendy. 'Live with Dad, and not with you.'

'What did you say?' asks Anne, trying to sound casual.

'I said no thank you,' says Wendy. 'There's no peace over there. They always have the builders in. Bang, bang, bang! And Dad's always shut away in a room, writing. I prefer it here, in spite of everything. Damp and draughts and all.'

The damp on the wall between the barred windows is worse. It makes a strange shape on the wall; it seems to change from day to day. The house belongs to Maurice. He will not have the roof over their heads mended. He says he cannot afford to. In the rooms above live tenants, protected by law, who pay next to nothing in rent. How can he spare the money needed to keep the house in good order – and why, according to Vanessa, should he?

'We're just the rejects of the world,' says Anne to Wendy, and Wendy believes her, and her mouth grows tight and pouty instead of firm and generous, as it could have been, and her looks are spoiled. Anne is right, that's the trouble of it. Rejects!

'How my shoulder hurts,' says Anne. She should have stayed at home, never crossed the city to stand beneath the plane tree in the alley behind Aldermans Drive, allowed herself her paroxysms of jealousy, grief, and solitary sexual frenzy.

She has had fibrositis ever since. But she felt what she felt. You can help what you do, but not what you feel.

The ghost looks further forward to Aldermans Drive and finds the bed gone in the small back room, and a dining table in its place, and candles lit, and guests, and smooth mushroom soup being served. The candles throw shadows on to the wall: this way, that way. One of the guests tries to make sense of them, but can't. She has wild blonde hair and a fair skin and a laughing mouth, unlike Maurice's other women. Her name is Audrey. She is an actress. Maurice's hair is falling out. His temples are quite bare, and he has a moustache now instead of a beard, and he seems distinguished, rather than aspiring. His hand smoothes Audrey's little one, and Vanessa sees. Maurice defies her jealousy: he smiles blandly, cruelly, at his wife.

He turns to Audrey's husband, who is eighteen years older than Audrey, and says, 'Ah youth, youth!' and offers back Audrey's hand, closing the husband's fingers over the wife's so that nobody could possibly take offence, and Vanessa feels puzzled at her own distress, and her glass of red wine tips over on its own account.

'Vanessa! Clumsy!' reproaches Maurice.
'But I didn't!' she says. No one believes her. Why should they? They pour white wine on the stain to neutralise the red, and it works, and looking at the tablecloth, presently, no one would have known anything untoward had happened at all.

'We must have security,' Vanessa weeps from time to time. 'I can't stand the uncertainty of it all! You must stop being

a writer. Or write something different. Stop writing novels.
Write for television instead.'
'No, you must stop spending the money,' he shouts. 'Stop
doing up this house. Changing this, changing that.'
'But I want it to be nice. We must have a nursery. I can't
keep the baby in a drawer.'
Vanessa is pregnant.
'Why not? It's what Anne had to do, thanks to you.'
'Anne! Can't you ever forget Anne?' she shrieks. 'Does she
have to be on our backs for ever? She has ruined our lives.'

But their lives aren't ruined. The small back room becomes
a nursery. The baby sleeps there. He is a boy, his name is
Jonathan. He sleeps badly and cries a lot and is hard to
love. His eyes follow the shadows on the wall, this way,
that way.

'There's nothing wrong with his eyes,' says the doctor, vis-
iting, puzzled at the mother's fears. 'But his chest is bad.'

Vanessa sits by the cot and rocks her feverish child.
'For you and I –' she sings, as she sings when she is nervous,
driving away fear with melody –
'– have a guardian angel – on high with nothing to do –
but to give to you and to give – to me – love for ever
– true –.'

Maurice is in the room. Vanessa is crying.
'But why won't you go back to work?' he demands. 'It would
take the pressure off me. I could write what I want to write,
not what I have to write.'
'I want to look after my baby myself,' she weeps. 'It's a man's
job to support his family. And you're not exactly William

Shakespeare. Why don't you write films? That's where the money is.'

The baby coughs. The doctor says the room is too damp for its good.
'I never liked this room,' says Vanessa, as she and Maurice carry out the cot. 'And you and I always quarrel in it. The quarrelling room. I hate it. But I love you.'
'I love you,' he says, crossing his fingers.

The ghost looks forward. Aldermans Drive has become one of the most desirable streets in Bristol, all new paint and French kitchenware and Welsh dressers seen through lighted windows. The property is in Maurice's name, as seems reasonable, since he earns the money. He writes films, for Hollywood.

Anne's bed turns into a foam settee by day: she has a cooker instead of a gas ring: the window bars have gone: the panes are made of reinforced glass. She has had a telephone installed. Wendy has platform heels and puts cream on her spots.

The ghost looks further forward, and Anne has a boyfriend. A man sits opposite her in a freshly covered armchair. Broken springs have been taped flat. Sometimes she lets him into her bed, but his flesh is cool and none too firm, and she remembers Maurice's body, hot-water bottle in her bed, and won't forget. Won't. Can't.

'Is it wrong to hate people?' asks Anne. 'I hate Vanessa, and with reason. She is a thief. Why do people ask her into their houses? Is it that they don't realise, or just that they don't

184

care? She stole my husband: she tried to steal my child. Maurice has never been happy with her. He never wanted to leave me. She seduced him. She thought he'd be famous one day; how wrong she was! He's sold out, you know! One day he'll come back to me, what's left of him, and I'll be expected to pick up the bits.'

'But he's married to her. They have a child. How can he come back to you?' He is a nice man, a salesman, thoughtful and kind.

'So was I married to him. So do I have his child.'

How stubborn she is!

'You're obsessive.' He is beginning to be angry. Well, he has been angry often enough before, and still stayed around for more. 'While you take Maurice's money,' he says, 'you will never be free of him.'

'Those few miserable pennies! What difference can they make? I live in penury, while she lives in style. He is Wendy's father; he has an obligation to support us. He was the guilty party, after all.'

'The law no longer says guilty or not guilty, in matter of divorce.'

'Well, it should!' She is passionate. 'He should pay for what he did to me and Wendy. He destroyed our lives.'

The ghost is lulled by the turning wheel of her thoughts, so steady on its axis: he drowses; responds to a spasm of despair, an act of decision on the man's part, one morning, as he leaves Anne's unsatisfactory bed. He dresses silently: he means to go: never to come back. He looks in the mirror to straighten his tie and sees Anne's face instead of his own.

He cries out and Anne wakes.

'I'm sorry,' she says. 'Don't go.'

But he does, and he doesn't come back.
The gap between what could be, and what is, defeats him.

Anne has a job as a waitress. It is a humiliation. Maurice
does not know she is earning. Anne keeps it a secret, for
Vanessa would surely love an excuse to reduce Anne's
alimony, already whittled away by inflation.

The decorators are back in Aldermans Drive. The smell of
fresh plaster has the ghost alert. Paper is being stripped from
walls: doors driven through here: walls dismantled there.
The cat runs before the ghost, like a leaf before wind, looking
for escape; finding none, cornered in the small back room,
where animals never go if they can help it, and the shadows
swing to and fro, and the tiny crossed bones from a dead
sparrow are lodged beneath the wainscot.

'Get out of here, cat!' cries Vanessa. 'I hate cats, don't you?
Maurice loves them. But they don't like me: for ever trying
to trip me on the stairs, when I had to go to the baby, in
the night.'

'I expect they were jealous,' says the man with her. He is
young and handsome, with shrewd, insincere eyes and a
lecher's mouth. He is a decorator. He looks at the room
with dislike, and at Vanessa, speculatively.

'The worst room in the house,' she laments. 'It's been
bedroom, dining room, nursery. It never works! I hope it's
better as a bathroom.'

He moves his hand to the back of her neck but she laughs
and sidesteps.

'The plaster's shockingly damp,' he says, and as if to prove his opinion the curtain rail falls off the wall altogether, making a terrible clatter and clash, and the cat yowls and Vanessa shrieks, and Maurice strides up the stairs to see what is happening, and what was in the air between Vanessa and Toby evaporates. The ghost is on Anne's side — if ghosts take sides.

How grand and boring the house is now! There is a faint scent of chlorine in the air; it comes from the swimming pool in the basement. The stair walls are mirrored: a maid polishes away at the first landing but it's always a little misty. She marvels at how long the flowers last, when placed on the little Georgian stair-table brought by Vanessa for Maurice on his fifty-second birthday. The maid is in love with Maurice, but Maurice has other fish to fry.

Further forward still: something's happening in the bathroom! The bath is deep blue and the taps are gold, and the wallpaper rose, but still the shadows swing to and fro, against the wall.
Audrey has spilt red wine upon her dress. She is more beautiful than she was. She is intelligent. She is no longer married or an actress: she is a solicitor. Maurice admires that very much. He thinks women should be useful, not like Vanessa. He is tired of girls who have young flesh and liquid eyes and love his bed but despise him in their hearts. Audrey does not despise him. Vanessa has forgotten how.

Maurice is helping Audrey sponge down her dress. His hand strays here and there. She is accustomed to it: she does not mind.
'What are those shadows on the wall?' she asks.

'Some trick of the light,' he says.

'Perhaps we should use white wine to remove the red,' she says. 'Remember that night so long ago? It was in this room, wasn't it! Vanessa had it as a dining room, then. I think I fell in love with you that night.'

'And I with you,' he says.

Is it true? – He can hardly remember.

'What a lot of time we've wasted,' he laments, and this for both of them is true enough. They love each other.

'Dear Maurice,' she says, 'I can't bear to see you so unhappy. It's all Vanessa's doing. She stopped you writing. You would be a great writer if it wasn't for her, not just a Hollywood hack! You still could be!'

He laughs, but he is moved. He thinks it might be true. If it were not for Vanessa he would not just be rich and successful, he would be rich, successful and renowned as well.

'Vanessa says this room is haunted,' he says, seeing the shadows himself, almost defined at last, a body hanging from a noose: a woman destroyed, or self-destroyed. What's the difference? Love does it. Love and ghosts.

'What's the matter?' Audrey asks. He's pale.

'We could leave here,' he says. 'Leave this house. You and me.'

A shrewd light gleams in her intelligent, passionate eyes. How he loves her!

'A pity to waste all this,' says Audrey. 'It is your home, after all. Vanessa's never liked it. If anyone leaves, it should be her.'

The flowers on the landing are still fresh and sweet a week

188

later. Maurice will keep the table they stand upon – a gift from Vanessa to him, after all. If you give someone something, it's theirs for ever. That is the law, says Audrey.

Vanessa moves her belongings from the bathroom shelf. She wants nothing of his, nothing. Just a few personal things – toothbrush, paste, cleansing cream. She will take her child and go. She cannot remain under the same roof, and he won't leave.

'You must see it's for the best, Vanessa,' says Maurice, awkwardly. 'We haven't really been together for years, you and I.'
'All that bed-sharing?' she enquires. 'That wasn't together? The meals, the holidays, the friends, the house? The child? Not together?'
'No,' he says. 'Not together the way I feel with Audrey.'
She can hardly believe it. So far she is shocked, rather than distressed. Presently, distress will set in: but not yet.

'I'll provide for you, of course,' he says, 'you and the child. I always looked after Anne, didn't I? Anne and Wendy.'
Vanessa turns to stare at him, and over his shoulder sees a dead woman hanging from a rope, but who is to say where dreams begin and reality ends? At the moment she is certainly in a nightmare. She looks back to Maurice, and sees the horror of her own life, and the swinging body fades, if indeed it was ever there. The door opens, by itself.
'You never did fix the catch,' she says.
'No,' he replies. 'I never got round to it.'

The train beneath the overpass was nearly through. The past had caught up with the present and the present was dissolving into the future, and the future was all but out of sight.

It was 1980. The two women, Anne and Vanessa, sat together in the room in Upton Park. The damp patch was back again, but hidden by one of the numerous posters which lined the walls calling on women to live, to be free, to protest, to reclaim the right, demand wages for housework, to do anything in the world but love. The personal, they proclaimed, was the political. Other women came and went in the room.

'However good the present is,' said Anne, 'the past cannot be undone. I wasted so much of my life. I look back and see scenes I would rather not remember. Little things; silly things, even. Wendy being late for school, a lover looking in a mirror. Damp on a wall. I used to think this room was haunted.'

'I used to think the same of Aldermans Drive,' said Vanessa, 'but now I realise what it was. What I sensed was myself now, looking back; me now watching me then, myself remembering me with sorrow for what I was and need never have been.'

They talked about Audrey.

'They say she's unfaithful to him,' said Anne. 'Well, he's nearly sixty and she's thirty-five. What did he expect?'

'Love,' said Vanessa, 'like the rest of us.'

Geoffrey and the Eskimo Child

Geoffrey thought that perhaps Tania should see a psychotherapist. She was having nightmares, the substance of which eluded her but the attendant feeling – tone (as she learned to call it) – being clear enough. Terror.

That was in 1962 and their joint income was low. Geoffrey was studying sociology at the London School of Economics, and Tania, who already had her degree, was working for a market research organisation in a rather humble capacity.

'Can we afford it?' mourned Tania. 'Isn't psychotherapy an unimaginable luxury? Isn't it immoral to accept a form of treatment which can never, by virtue of it being on a one-to-one basis, be available to the many, but only to the privileged few?' She was very earnest, in those days.

Geoffrey reasoned that if Tania needed psychotherapy she should have it: that her happiness was important to him: that she was a valuable member of the community and would be able to pass on the benefit of self-awareness to many others in the course of her life. Their children, too, would benefit, when the time came to have them. Psychotherapy was like a stone dropping into a pool: the ripples spread and spread, with an ever widening circumference.

'Can't you make up your own mind, Tania?' asked Erica. 'Do you always have to ask Geoffrey what to do?' But it seemed that Tania did. Erica was Tania's friend. Once Erica had been Geoffrey's mistress, but that was long ago. Now she did not seem to like Geoffrey very much, so Tania did not pay attention to those parts of Erica's conversation which appertained to her husband.

Geoffrey drove Tania to the psychotherapist for the initial visit, and took her out for a drink afterwards, and was rather nonplussed when she didn't tell him what had passed between the psychotherapist and herself. However, being reasonable and kind, he did not press the matter but allowed his wife her privacy.

'We can be one flesh,' he acknowledged, 'but we have to remain two minds. Otherwise, where's the mutual benefit, and stimulation? The cross-fertilisation?'

'I'm on the pill,' Tania had remarked to the therapist, who was a pleasant woman.
'What pill?'
'The contraceptive pill,' Tania had replied, and explained all about it. It had been tried out on Puerto Rican women and proved safe. The therapist had seemed rather baffled by this new development in the world, of which so far she had apparently been unaware, but was able nevertheless to relate Tania's nightly terrors to the nightly taking of the pill and the denial of her own femininity, and fear of ensuing punishment.

Tania did not, and could not, accept such an absurd explanation, and presently stopped her visits. She went on taking the pill, and the nightmares faded, and were forgotten, absorbed into the past along with everything else.

Geoffrey got a First and was rewarded with a rather insecure job as a junior lecturer at the London School of Economics. He was a Marxist, but of the stable kind which never degenerates into Trotskyism or Maoism, and his seniors believed that with time he would grow out of even that. Tania went into journalism. More money now came into the household, but both had spendthrift habits and neither approved of private property anyway, so they did not buy a house but continued to live in rented accommodation. Geoffrey spent a proportion of their joint income each year equipping sports halls for the local skinheads. 'We have everything we need,' he said, 'and these lads have nothing.'
'God, Geoffrey's a fool!' said Erica. Tania did not have her in the house for quite some time.

Geoffrey and Tania put off having children. Time enough for that. Tania stayed on the pill, year in, year out, through health scares and out the other side of them, with regular physical check-ups and the dosage changing for maximum safety. Geoffrey saw to that.
'Contraception is both our responsibility,' said Geoffrey. He was an orphan himself: he wanted children, but not until Tania was ready.

Even as far back as 1968, when the whole Western world was gasping, heaving, and setting off in a different direction, in hot pursuit of youth, Geoffrey was conscious of the unfairness of woman's lot in society. In *his* revolutionary meetings, men were expected to make the coffee too, and women allowed to make policy decisions. And when the Women's Movement started, Geoffrey helped with the general organisation and setting up of meetings and the printing of pamphlets, and tried to deter his fellow men from standing up first when discussion time came, and the platform had finished, and prefixing their remarks with – 'I'm all for Women's Liberation. I always help my wife with the washing up.'

'I *do* the washing up,' said Geoffrey. 'We share household chores. We split our lives down the middle. When we have children – a pigeon pair would be nice: a boy and a girl, and then I'll have a vasectomy – it will be the same. We will take turns at tribulation as well as joy. We will share the chores of earning, cooking, washing, bill-paying, hoovering, cleaning the lavatory. All men should act likewise!'

Tania was thirty-two. It was no longer possible to deny that she was growing older, and that giving birth to a first child no longer the simple matter it once would have been. And man's procreative life, of course, goes on longer than woman's, and male sperm, being re-created daily, do not grow feeble or tired, as do female eggs, which are laid down before birth and have to hang about for release – and the danger of having a baby with something wrong with it presumably increased with every year that passed.

'Poppycock!' murmured Erica when Tania announced that time had run out and that she was coming off the pill. 'If doctors can't think of one way to frighten women, they'll think of another.' But no one listened to Erica. She disliked babies and had no intention of ever having one. She boasted of having had three terminations.

There were other worries, too. There was so much to be done in the world, and so many people in it, were they *entitled* to have children? Was the world a fit place to bring children into? This latter was Tania's worry. Geoffrey's, freely expressed, was whether, when it came to actuality and not just declamation, their domestic sharing, which worked so well without children, would continue to work when a child arrived? Or, if there was any conflict of interest, say an ill child needing a parent to stay home, which parent would it be? Geoffrey now had a job as a sociologist at the Camden Town Hall and was in charge of a department, which he ran with enthusiasm and energy, cutting away – perhaps a little ruthlessly – the dead wood of old staff and old ideas. He was relentlessly *young*; he wore jeans to work before anyone else dared, and had already abandoned collar and tie when others were still cautiously wondering if they could possibly abandon their vests. Tania had become a freelance journalist of note: she was a leading member of Women in Media: and an expert in women's affairs.

'Obviously,' said Geoffrey, 'I have a department to run, and you, Tania, can be flexible in your working arrangements, but that is hardly the point!'

'We'll work it out somehow,' said Tania, throwing away her pills. 'It's a matter of the efficient division of labour, that's all. We'll each do the best we can!'

Tania was much envied by her friends and colleagues, inasmuch as she was married to Geoffrey, who was one of the few genuinely un-chauvinist men around, was not impotent but nevertheless apparently monogamous, and wasn't even boring. Geoffrey's mind worked marvellously, his tongue freely, and he passed lightly over this subject and that, seeming to know everything and everyone, lighting up rooms as he came into them. He could make people laugh, with his mock macho stances: he could listen quietly and at length if he had to, and his interest in others was genuine, and profound. He kept his fits of melancholy for home, and warned Tania when they were coming, so she could go away for a couple of days if they were bad, or just to the pictures if it was a transitory mood and not likely to outlast the evening. In these gloomy states, he was angry and rejecting of her: reproaches and rebukes sparking out of black silence. Tania had long since learned to discount them: not to include them in her vision of him, beloved Geoffrey, her good husband.

Both Tania and Geoffrey were surprised when Tania did not get pregnant at once. Tania was perhaps, for a month or so, secretly a little relieved. Relief quickly faded, to be replaced by a nagging anxiety. They were disconcerted to be told, by friends, that her fertility might not reassert itself for a year or so, and they saw themselves now in a race against time. Every month that passed seemed to increase the danger both to Tania and to the as yet unconceived baby, which now seemed as real as they were – a gap in the room where a highchair should be, a space in the hall where there was no pram.

After a year of trying to become pregnant, and failing, Tania visited the staff doctor at the newspaper where she worked. He explained that five per cent of couples are sterile, a problem masked for women who had been taking

196

the contraceptive pill since the beginning of their sexual relationships. He was not suggesting Tania was infertile, simply saying it was a possibility which must be faced.

'Good God,' protested Geoffrey, 'it might be *me* who's infertile (he hasn't even considered that); the man's a cretin!'

After much discussion as to the rights and wrongs of such a step, Tania agreed to visit a doctor in private practice, who had a more enlightened view of conception.

'It's always a conflict between individual right and public good,' Tania tried to explain to Erica, but Erica had no time for such excuses.

'It always happens,' lamented Erica. 'The drift to the right as people grow older!' Erica had no sympathy for Tania's pale face and haunted eyes, and Geoffrey's new quietness of demeanour, as month succeeded month, Tania's blood flowed, and disappointment and a sense of failure ensued in both of them. Geoffrey had no family himself, having been brought up by a solitary aunt. Tania's elderly father made up all of her relatives. He and she perched, being without children, on a dead branch of a family tree, and it crackled with misery.

Geoffrey's sperm count was normal; there was no apparent reason for Tania's failure to conceive. She had her fallopian tubes blown up with air – a rather disagreeable and expensive operation: she took pills to increase her fertility, which also increased her chances of multiple birth, but these measures did not work. She and Geoffrey confined intercourse to days of the month when she was most likely to conceive: she took Vitamin E, drank rosehip tea, and went to a hypnotist and after that an acupuncturist, all to no avail. Her body maintained the relentless, pulsing, bleeding course it had become so accustomed to.

When Tania was thirty-six, and worn out by hope disappointed, she gave up. 'I shall be an aunt,' she said, 'everyone's favourite aunt, since nature insists I cannot be a mother. And besides, there are certainly more than enough children in the world already, and quite enough work to be getting on with.'

Geoffrey and she agreed that the world was in a perilous state: cadmium in the fish, lead in the water, and radiation in the very air you breathed, and they concentrated their talents and energies into making it a safer place for future generations. It seemed a noble enough task.

Tania was offered the editorship of the newspaper.
'We must consider this really carefully,' said Geoffrey. 'It does mean a total commitment on your part. Is this what you really want from your life? Or perhaps it's time now for us to have a little rest and relaxation? You are looking rather tired, these days.'

Geoffrey was on a strict and successful diet. His jeans met easily enough. He still had all his hair. He looked ten years younger than his age: Tania looked perhaps a year or two older than hers, and had a tendency to eat cream eclairs and put sugar in her coffee.
'You must stop this consolation eating,' said Erica, who was thin and muscly. 'It is obscene for someone as fortunate as you to need consolation,' and Tania realised the truth of this, lost a stone, and was herself again.

Tania turned down the editorship and she and Geoffrey adopted a half-Vietnamese half-American little girl, aged four when they first saw her, and five when they took possession of her. In the interval, the delicate Vietnamese features Geoffrey had so loved seemed to have given way to a certain American jowliness and clumsiness. But Tania loved her. They named her Star. In the interval, too, Tania became pregnant and gave birth to identical girl twins.

'You should never have taken the fertility pill,' said Erica. 'Two! It's unnatural! Monozygotic – more of a mutation than anything else!'
The doctor – their local GP and not one in private practice, for care of three children was expensive, and the whole family now had to live on one salary, Geoffrey's, instead of two – said, 'Nonsense! A completely random chance. Nothing to do with the fertility drug at all,' and might have been right, for all anyone knew.

It was out of the question for Geoffrey to share household chores; it took him all his energy to bring in enough money to keep the household going. It was out of the question for Tania to earn; one disturbed five-year-old (little Star lied, fought and stole, and had to have the reassurance of Tania's constant attention) and twin babies took up all her time and energy.
'I knew you'd both revert to type,' said Erica, and Tania wished she'd go away. It was not as if Erica ever washed out a bottle or offered to soothe a crying infant. All she seemed to do was pop round when Tania was feeding Sally and Susan and ask Geoffrey round to the pub for a drink. He'd go, too.

'Of course Erica has turned lesbian,' he said, eventually. 'Well, I can understand that. Why should a woman make do with a man, when she can have another woman?'

And Erica faded out of the picture. Well, is there a marriage in the world in which each partner is for ever true, in word, deed and fantasy, to the other?

The world outside continued to deteriorate. Oil prices soared: energy crises ensued: police states threatened, at home and abroad: certifiable madmen headed previously dignified states: even Geoffrey's job looked not so secure as before. But Tania was happy enough with her family.

'We must look after the next generation,' said Geoffrey, when Star was nine and the twins were four. 'It's all we can do for the world. We must adopt a child whom no one else wants.'

'Can we afford it?'

'Good heavens,' said Geoffrey. 'Families of nine manage very well on half what I earn!'

'But it's so nice,' said Tania, 'to have everyone out of nappies, and just a little time to myself.'

'Darling,' said Geoffrey, 'I know what it's like for you. Any time you want, I'll stay home and look after the kids while you go out to work. I'm pretty tired of the rat-race, I can tell you.'

'I don't know,' said Tania doubtfully. 'I seem to have rather got out of the way of things. And where would I find a job that paid as much as yours, or had such nice long holidays? No, things are pretty good as they are. We'll carry on a little longer.'

Geoffrey quickly took Tania to a children's home to see a

child who had passed through his office files, and was being put up for adoption. She was the prettiest, blondest, most delicate little creature ever put in care, said Geoffrey, and Tania was obliged to agree. Her name was Jenny. She was six. She smiled at Geoffrey and looked coldly at Tania.

'Oh Geoffrey, we can't,' cried Tania, having woken in the middle of that night from a recurrence of her old trouble – nightmares. 'It will upset Star too much and make the twins jealous. An older or a younger child, but not one in the middle, please. Not a blonde, when the others are so dark, not a girl, when we have three girls already, and not a girl with this particular history, and most of all not *now*.'

'Night fears!' said Geoffrey. 'Perhaps you should try primal scream therapy?'

But Tania now hardly had the time, let alone the energy, to scream. They took in little Jenny who had remained un-snapped up by adoptors, in spite of her prettiness, because of her psychiatric history. She was mildly autistic, given to sudden shouts and fits of swearing and aggression, and her very presence in the house made Star revert to her earlier state of distress and the twins to adopt an irritating private language of their own. Tania, by dedication and with help from Geoffrey, had the household reasonably peaceful within six months, but was always aware of Jenny's hostility.

The night of the nightmare Tania must have conceived. Certainly the dates were about right, though why she should make a connection between the two events she was not quite sure. She was delighted to be pregnant, to have this second affirmation of her femininity after the dreadful years, and Geoffrey was proud as a peacock. He had not been able to have a vasectomy after all, because new evidence had come to light about possible side-effects and premature senility. Nor did she any longer wish vasectomy upon him. The long years of infertility had changed them both, made them value what they had together, and given an underlying seriousness to the act of sex.

They even discussed the possibility of becoming Catholics. They understood the Pope's stand on contraception, but could not quite accept the doctrine of the Assumption of the Virgin Mary, and so did not in the end undergo conversion.

'Anyway,' said Tania, 'your work colleagues would laugh at you. I'm sure they're all atheists!'
'Atheists, vedantists, Marxists and idiots,' said Geoffrey. He was disenchanted with work.

There was quite a scare when it looked as if Tania was having twins again, but it did not happen. She gave birth to a son, Simon. But something rather strange happened to her insides at the same time – perhaps the earlier blowing and scraping and medicating was to blame, although the doctor laughed and said nonsense – but at any rate Tania was told she would not be able to conceive any more, and would do well to have a hysterectomy.

Geoffrey cried, and Tania put it off as long as she could, but in the end the strain of losing blood, and the care of five children, two of them disturbed and one of them a baby, told too much, and she had her hysterectomy. The event seemed to depress Geoffrey very much. His moodiness got worse, and he did not even bother to take it to the pub, out of Tania's way. He worried more and more about the lead, the strontium, the ozone layer, earthquakes, volcanoes, the government, plots against him at work and the onset of nuclear war, and received an offer of redundancy pay from his employers, which he hotly and bitterly declined.

Tania went on looking after the children.

Simon grew to be a lively, clever child, but Geoffrey saw signs of doom written in his eyes, and when Tania was forty-three, and Simon two, he said it was time to adopt another child.

'Oh no, oh no!' begged Tania. She was worried about a swollen vein in her leg, and thought it might be the beginning of a varicose vein.

'Good God,' said Geoffrey, 'you're lucky to have a leg! Lots of people don't even have legs to have varicose veins in!' and Tania was obliged to admit it was true.

She did a lot of walking and lugging shopping about. They had sold the car because it was polluting the air with lead fumes, and adding to the general distress of the world.

'I don't think anyone's going to let us adopt a child,' said Tania, firmly. 'Anyone in their right mind would say we had enough!'

She mourned the loss of that female part of her which seemed to have gone with her womb. She felt strange without it: a person. And though Geoffrey told her that was what everyone must try to be, a person, except in bed when you were allowed to be male or female, she was not altogether comforted. She had hormone therapy now, to counteract the effect of being without a womb, and took oestrogen by mouth again, as once she had before, in her young, carefree days, when she did what she wanted, and not what she had to.

Geoffrey asked around, and indeed, it looked as if another adoption would be hard to arrange, even if they undertook to take in a deviant fourteen-year-old male half-caste, the most difficult kind of child to place.

He felt it was Tania's fault.
'You sit there at these interviews looking tired and exhausted on purpose,' he said. 'I'm sure you do. It's unconscious, of course. I'm not accusing you of open negativism, but the results are the same. Poor little Simon has to have a brother. The only boy! He's going to be so lonely, and have trouble with his role identification.'
'He can identify with me,' said Tania. 'I'm a person, aren't I?' She tried not to make remarks like this, but at the time Star was staying out all night and Jenny had reverted to wetting the bed and biting the sheets to ribbons and the twins were playing truant from school and she was tired.

'Education is the prison of the mind,' said Geoffrey, who seemed unalarmed by such symptoms, 'the twins are show-ing courage and sense in staying away from their school!'

Tania wondered if it were so: she still saw their way ahead as she had her own – through the educational system and the passing of examinations, to the pinnacle of free thought and the free expression of that thought. As for helping the less advantaged members of the community, Geoffrey did that on a large scale, she on an individual one. Well, that was how it went: how it had turned out.

She knew that Geoffrey was right: she saw that while she had life and strength and good-will she must feed it back, in her small way, into the community. How else was the world to be saved?

But she knew that to bring another child into the family would do little Simon no good at all. He was the youngest; her perfect son; passionately she wished him a safe and peaceful upbringing.

'Tania,' said Geoffrey, 'if everyone of goodwill doesn't do their utmost now, there won't be a world to bring him up in!'

The nuclear threat hung over him like a cloud. Erica made a brief appearance.
'One would almost think Geoffrey was earmarked for his own personal missile,' she whispered, in a voice grown impossibly soft and sexy. She seemed less muscly and athletic as she grew older: just rather slender and vulnerable. She had time to paint her toenails. She hadn't veered to the political right with age, just to the soft left of the women's movement. No truck there with the separatists, those who looked ahead to a world without men.

Geoffrey explained to Erica how the war between good and evil was hotting up, and how all those on the side of good must be very, very busy indeed about their business.

'You really ought to try and cheer him up, Tania,' said Erica. She was mysterious about her own life, but Tania had the distinct feeling she was heterosexual again. She herself remained, perforce, very much a person. Geoffrey

205

had rather gone off sex, lately. Their nights were usually disturbed by one or other of the five children, and sleep seemed the highest pleasure.

But Geoffrey did not give up the thought of adopting another child.

'The balance of the household isn't right,' he complained. 'I can feel it isn't. We must have another boy, and you don't have the wherewithal any more to provide one yourself. Tania, I'll help you with everything. You know I will.'

'You're very good,' said Tania. 'You always help with the washing up!'

He lay awake wondering how to acquire a baby. She had nightmares, again. What had the psychotherapist said, long, long ago? The daily denial of femininity? It began to make sense. She took another oestrogen pill. If ever she forgot, she had hot flushes and became depressed.

'Have I ever before asked you to make a sacrifice for me?' asked Geoffrey. 'I'm asking you, begging you, now, in the name of our love, and everything we have struggled for together: our common beliefs and aspirations. You in your way, I in mine. We must have another son!'

Tania gave in. One day shortly afterwards Geoffrey came home from work in the middle of the day, carrying an Eskimo baby, two hours old.

'Eskimo!' exclaimed Tania, looking at the serene little face framed in its greyish open-mesh social-welfare blanket, as Geoffrey handed the infant to her.

'It was meant,' said Geoffrey. 'It was a sign that I was right!

An Eskimo – one of the most oppressed and endangered human species in the world!'

If you have been married for a long, long time, what seems strange to the outside world seems quite normal to husband and wife. Tania could accept Geoffrey's reasoning. She could see that it was *meant*.

God's will, that a pregnant Eskimo girl should stow away in a crate of scientific instruments on an aircraft bound from Alaska to Heathrow. God's will that by a series of miracles she and the baby should survive, should end up in the vast offices of Camden Social Services, that she should give birth, there and then, in the space of five minutes, to a healthy nine-pound baby boy, hand the baby to Geoffrey, and die.

As Geoffrey had a wife at home ready and willing to look after a newborn baby, and the doctor said of course, any home was better than an institution for an orphaned baby and the sooner he was in a woman's arms the better, Geoffrey left with the baby as the undertaker arrived.

The Social Services department was like that, said Geoffrey. Sometimes nothing seemed to happen for weeks – then everything all at once.

Tania reared the Eskimo baby, and thought perhaps Geoffrey had been right. The presence of this particular child seemed to soothe the others. Geoffrey remained moody and ready to blame, however.

When the baby was a year old he determined to take them all on holiday in Crete. Tania was at first dubious of the wisdom of such a plan but Geoffrey persisted and presently she and the children were looking forward to the holiday, with happiness and animation. The money spent on the holiday had nearly been spent on a nuclear shelter. It had been a toss-up. Not quite a toss-up: Geoffrey had held out his clenched fists to the Eskimo baby; one hand was marked Shelter, and the child had chosen Holiday.

It took Tania a week to prepare for the journey. The requisites of six children require a good deal of parental organising, although Geoffrey did what he could to help. They were to drive to the airport, and be there by two. At twenty past twelve Star discovered she had started her first period, to Sally and Susan's consternation. The party's departure was delayed by fifteen minutes, which meant that Geoffrey would have to drive fast to the airport to make up for lost time, but he did not seem particularly disconcerted. When the family was re-settled nicely in the car, and the engine started, Geoffrey seemed to remember something, switched off the engine, said 'Just a minute,' and went inside.

Fifteen minutes later, as he had not returned, Tania disentangled herself from various living limbs and went to look for him. She found him in the back garden. He had shot himself dead, with a gun he should not have had.

She could give no explanation to the coroner: she could give no explanation to herself. Geoffrey had drifted into some kind of melancholy, she supposed, so gradually that she had not noticed. Perhaps if she had, she could have saved him? But she had been busy, she tried to excuse herself; and about his business, more than her own. No one seemed inclined to blame her, so she blamed herself. There was no insurance, no property, just six children and rent to be paid.

Tania worried in case Geoffrey could not, as a suicide, be buried in consecrated ground, but there seemed no longer any time or indeed opportunity for such worry at the great overworked institutions which look after the disposal of the dead. He had once said, in joking casual conversation, that he wanted to be burned *and* buried, so she arranged for his cremation and the burial of his ashes.

There was quite a large gathering around the open grave, as the coffin containing the casket was lowered into the ground. (This particular bureaucracy, too, worked in strange ways: easier to go along with it than arrange for a rational casket-size coffin.) For a child who had started out an orphan, Geoffrey had accumulated a large family of friends, colleagues and relatives. It had been a successful life, so far as it had gone. Erica was there, by the graveside, with a year-old baby in her arms. If the child looked like Geoffrey, and Tania rather thought it might, it seemed not to matter.

She looked at her children – at Star, Susan, Sally, Jenny and Simon, and at the stocky little baby who rested placidly on her hip, and wondered what was to become of them all.

'Geoffrey,' she asked in her heart, into the still, sniffy quiet around the grave, as the first token lumps of soil were thrown, 'what am I going to do now?'
But Geoffrey didn't reply.

Weekend

By seven-thirty they were ready to go. Martha had everything packed into the car and the three children appropri-
ately dressed and in the back seat, complete with educational
games and wholewheat biscuits. When everything was ready
in the car Martin would switch off the television, come
downstairs, lock up the house, front and back, and take
the wheel.

Weekend! Only two hours' drive down to the cottage on
Friday evenings: three hours' drive back on Sunday nights.
The pleasures of greenery and guests in between. They
reckoned themselves fortunate, how fortunate!

On Fridays Martha would get home on the bus at six-twelve
and prepare tea and sandwiches for the family: then she
would strip four beds and put the sheets and quilt covers in
the washing machine for Monday: take the country bedding
from the airing basket, plus the books and the games, plus
the weekend food – acquired at intervals throughout the
week, to lessen the load – plus her own folder of work from
the office, plus Martin's drawing materials (she was a market
researcher in an advertising agency, he a freelance designer)
plus hairbrushes, jeans, spare T-shirts, Jolyon's antibiotics

(he suffered from sore throats), Jenny's recorder, Jasper's cassette player and so on – ah, the so on! – and would pack them all, skilfully and quickly, into the boot. Very little could be left in the cottage during the week. ('An open invitation to burglars': Martin) Then Martha would run round the house tidying and wiping, doing this and that, finding the cat at one neighbour's and delivering it to another, while the others ate their tea; and would usually, proudly, have everything finished by the time they had eaten their fill. Martin would just catch the BBC2 news, while Martha cleared away the tea table, and the children tossed up for the best positions in the car. 'Martha,' said Martin, tonight, 'you ought to get Mrs Hodder to do more. She takes advantage of you.'

Mrs Hodder came in twice a week to clean. She was over seventy. She charged two pounds an hour. Martha paid her out of her own wages: well, the running of the house was Martha's concern. If Martha chose to go out to work – as was her perfect right, Martin allowed, even though it wasn't the best thing for the children, but that must be Martha's moral responsibility – Martha must surely pay her domestic stand-in. An evident truth, heard loud and clear and frequent in Martin's mouth and Martha's heart.

'I expect you're right,' said Martha. She did not want to argue. Martin had had a long hard week, and now had to drive. Martha couldn't. Martha's licence had been suspended four months back for drunken driving. Everyone agreed that the suspension was unfair: Martha seldom drank to excess: she was for one thing usually too busy pouring drinks for other people or washing other people's glasses to get much inside herself. But Martin had taken her out to dinner on her

211

birthday, as was his custom, and exhaustion and excitement mixed had made her imprudent, and before she knew where she was, why there she was, in the dock, with a distorted lamppost to pay for and a new bonnet for the car and six months' suspension.

So now Martin had to drive her car down to the cottage, and he was always tired on Fridays, and hot and sleepy on Sundays, and every rattle and clank and bump in the engine she felt to be somehow her fault.

Martin had a little sports car for London and work: it could nip in and out of the traffic nicely: Martha's was an old estate car, with room for the children, picnic baskets, bedding, food, games, plants, drink, portable television and all the things required by the middle classes for weekends in the country. It lumbered rather than zipped and made Martin angry. He seldom spoke a harsh word, but Martha, after the fashion of wives, could detect his mood from what he did not say rather than what he did, and from the tilt of his head, and the way his crinkly, merry eyes seemed crinklier and merrier still – and of course from the way he addressed Martha's car.

'Come along, you old banger you! Can't you do better than that? You're too old, that's your trouble. Stop complaining. Always complaining, it's only a hill. You're too wide about the hips. You'll never get through there.'

Martha worried about her age, her tendency to complain, and the width of her hips. She took the remarks personally. Was she right to do so? The children noticed nothing: it was just funny lively laughing Daddy being witty about Mummy's

212

car. Mummy, done for drunken driving. Mummy, with the roots of melancholy somewhere deep beneath the bustling, busy, everyday self. Busy: ah so busy!

Martin would only laugh if she said anything about the way he spoke to her car and warn her against paranoia. 'Don't get like your mother, darling.' Martha's mother had, towards the end, thought that people were plotting against her. Martha's mother had led a secluded, suspicious life, and made Martha's childhood a chilly and a lonely time. Life now, by comparison, was wonderful for Martha. People, children, houses, conversations, food, drink, theatres – even, now, a career. Martin standing between her and the hostility of the world – popular, easy, funny Martin, beckoning the rest of the world into earshot.

Ah, she was grateful: little earnest Martha, with her shy ways and her penchant for passing boring exams – how her life had blossomed out! Three children too – Jasper, Jenny and Jolyon – all with Martin's broad brow and open looks, and the confidence born of her love and care, and the work she had put into them since the dawning of their days.

Martin drives. Martha, for once, drowses.

The right food, the right words, the right play. Doctors for the tonsils: dentists for the molars. Confiscate guns: censor television: encourage creativity. Paints and paper to hand: books on the shelves: meetings with teachers. Music teachers. Dancing lessons. Parties. Friends to tea. School plays. Open days. Junior orchestra.

Martha is jolted awake. Traffic lights. Martin doesn't like Martha to sleep while he drives.

Clothes. Oh, clothes! Can't wear this: must wear that. Dress shops. Piles of clothes in corners: duly washed, but waiting to be ironed, waiting to be put away.

Get the piles off the floor, into the laundry baskets. Martin doesn't like a mess.

Creativity arises out of order, not chaos. Five years off work while the children were small: back to work with seniority lost. What, did you think something was for nothing? If you have children, mother, that is your reward. It lies not in the world.

Have you taken enough food? Always hard to judge.

Food. Oh, food! Shop in the lunch hour. Lug it all home. Cook for the freezer on Wednesday evenings while Martin is at his car maintenance evening class, and isn't there to notice you being unrestful. Martin likes you to sit down in the evenings. Fruit, meat, vegetables, flour for home-made bread. Well, shop bread is full of pollutants. Frozen food, even your own, loses flavour. Martin often remarks on it. Condiments. Everyone loves mango chutney. But the expense!

London Airport to the left. Look, look, children! Concorde? No, idiot, of course it isn't Concorde.

Ah, to be all things to all people: children, husband, employer, friends! It can be done: yes, it can: super woman.

214

Drink. Home-made wine. Why not? Elderberries grown thick and rich in London: and at least you know what's in it. Store it in high cupboards: lots of room: up and down the step-ladder. Careful! Don't slip. Don't break anything.

No such thing as an accident. Accidents are Freudian slips: they are wilful, bad-tempered things.

Martin can't bear bad temper. Martin likes slim ladies. Diet. Martin rather likes his secretary. Diet. Martin admires slim legs and big bosoms. How to achieve them both? Impossible. But try, oh try, to be what you ought to be, not what you are. Inside and out.

Martin brings back flowers and chocolates: whisks Martha off for holiday weekends. Wonderful! The best husband in the world: look into his crinkly, merry, gentle eyes; see it there. So the mouth slopes away into something of a pout. Never mind. Gaze into the eyes. Love. It must be love. You married him. *You*. Surely *you* deserve true love?

Salisbury Plain. Stonehenge. Look, children, look! Mother, we've seen Stonehenge a hundred times. Go back to sleep.

Cook! Ah cook. People love to come to Martin and Martha's dinners. Work it out in your head in the lunch hour. If you get in at six-twelve, you can seal the meat while you beat the egg white while you feed the cat while you lay the table while you string the beans while you set out the cheese, goat's cheese, Martin loves goat's cheese, Martha tries to like goat's cheese – oh, bed, sleep, peace, quiet.

Sex! Ah sex. Orgasm, please. Martin requires it. Well, so do you. And you don't want his secretary providing a passion you neglected to develop. Do you? Quick, quick, the cosmic bond. Love. Married love.

Secretary! Probably a vulgar suspicion: nothing more. Probably a fit of paranoia, à la mother, now dead and gone. At peace.
R.I.P.
Chilly, lonely mother, following her suspicions where they led.

Nearly there, children. Nearly in paradise, nearly at the cottage. Have another biscuit.

Real roses round the door.

Roses. Prune, weed, spray, feed, pick. Avoid thorns. One of Martin's few harsh words.

'Martha, you can't not want roses! What kind of person am I married to? An anti-rose personality?'

Green grass. Oh, God, grass. Grass must be mown. Restful lawns, daisies bobbing, buttercups glowing. Roses and grass and books. Books.

Please, Martin, do we have to have the two hundred books, mostly twenties' first editions, bought at Christie's book sale on one of your afternoons off? Books need dusting.

Roars of laughter from Martin, Jasper, Jenny and Jolyon. Mummy says we shouldn't have the books: books need dusting!

Roses, green grass, books and peace.

Martha woke up with a start when they got to the cottage, and gave a little shriek which made them all laugh. Mummy's waking shriek, they called it.

Then there was the car to unpack and the beds to make up, and the electricity to connect, and the supper to make, and the cobwebs to remove, while Martin made the fire. Then supper – pork chops in sweet and sour sauce ('Pork is such a *dull* meat if you don't cook it properly': Martin), green salad from the garden, or such green salad as the rabbits had left. ('Martha, did you really net them properly? Be honest, now!': Martin) and sauté potatoes. Mash is so stodgy and ordinary, and instant mash unthinkable. The children studied the night sky with the aid of their star map. Wonderful, rewarding children!

Then clear up the supper: set the dough to prove for the bread: Martin already in bed: exhausted by the drive and lighting the fire. ('Martha, we really ought to get the logs stacked properly. Get the children to do it, will you?': Martin) Sweep and tidy: get the TV aerial right. Turn up Jasper's jeans where he has trodden the hem undone. ('He can't go around like *that*, Martha. Not even Jasper': Martin)

Midnight. Good night. Weekend guests arriving in the morning. Seven for lunch and dinner on Saturday. Seven for Sunday breakfast, nine for Sunday lunch. ('Don't fuss, darling. You always make such a fuss': Martin) Oh, God, forgotten the garlic squeezer. That means ten minutes with the back of a spoon and salt. Well, who wants *lumps* of garlic? No one. Not Martin's guests. Martin said so. Sleep.

Colin and Katie. Colin is Martin's oldest friend. Katie is his new young wife. Janet, Colin's other, earlier wife, was Martha's friend. Janet was rather like Martha, quieter and duller than her husband. A nag and a drag, Martin rather thought, and said, and of course she'd let herself go, everyone agreed. No one exactly excused Colin for walking out, but you could see the temptation.

Katie versus Janet.

Katie was languid, beautiful and elegant. She drawled when she spoke. Her hands were expressive: her feet were little and female. She had no children.

Janet plodded round on very flat, rather large feet. There was something wrong with them. They turned out slightly when she walked. She had two children. She was, frankly, boring. But Martha liked her: when Janet came down to the cottage she would wash up. Not in the way that most guests washed up – washing dutifully and setting everything out on the draining board, but actually drying and putting away too. And Janet would wash the bath and get the children all sat down, with chairs for everyone, even the littlest, and keep them quiet and satisfied so the grown-ups – well, the men – could get on with their conversation and their jokes and their love of country weekends, while Janet stared into space, as if grateful for the rest, quite happy.

Janet would garden, too. Weed the strawberries, while the men went for their walk; her great feet standing firm and square and sometimes crushing a plant or so, but never mind, oh never mind. Lovely Janet; who understood.

Now Janet was gone and here was Katie.

Katie talked with the men and went for walks with the men, and moved her ashtray rather impatiently when Martha tried to clear the drinks round it.

Dishes were boring, Katie implied by her manner, and domesticity was boring, and anyone who bothered with that kind of thing was a fool. Like Martha. Ash should be allowed to stay where it was, even if it was in the butter, and conversations should never be interrupted.

Knock, knock. Katie and Colin arrived at one-fifteen on Saturday morning, just after Martha had got to bed. 'You don't mind? It was the moonlight. We couldn't resist it. You should have seen Stonehenge! We didn't disturb you? Such early birds!'

Martha rustled up a quick meal of omelettes. Saturday night's eggs. ('Martha makes a lovely omelette': Martin) ('Honey, make one of your mushroom omelettes: cook the mushrooms separately, remember, with lemon. Otherwise the water from the mushrooms gets into the egg, and spoils everything.') Sunday supper mushrooms. But ungracious to say anything.

Martin had revived wonderfully at the sight of Colin and Katie. He brought out the whisky bottle. Glasses. Ice. Jug for water. Wait. Wash up another sinkful, when they're finished. 2 a.m.

'Don't do it tonight, darling.'

'It'll only take a sec.' Bright smile, not a hint of self-pity. Self-pity can spoil everyone's weekend.

Martha knows that if breakfast for seven is to be manageable the sink must be cleared of dishes. A tricky meal, breakfast. Especially if bacon, eggs, and tomatoes must all be cooked in separate pans. ('Separate pans mean separate flavours!': Martin)

She is running around in her nightie. Now if that had been Katie – but there's something so *practical* about Martha. Reassuring, mind; but the skimpy nightie and the broad rump and the thirty-eight years are all rather embarrassing. Martha can see it in Colin and Katie's eyes. Martin's too. Martha wishes she did not see so much in other people's eyes. Her mother did, too. Dear, dead mother. Did I misjudge you?

This was the second weekend Katie had been down with Colin but without Janet. Colin was a photographer: Katie had been his accessoriser. First Colin and Janet: then Colin, Janet and Katie: now Colin and Katie!

Katie weeded with rubber gloves on and pulled out pansies in mistake for weeds and laughed and laughed along with everyone when her mistake was pointed out to her, but the pansies died. Well, Colin had become with the years fairly rich and fairly famous, and what does a fairly rich and famous man want with a wife like Janet when Katie is at hand?

On the first of the Colin/Janet/Katie weekends Katie had appeared out of the bathroom. 'I say,' said Katie, holding out a damp towel with evident distaste, 'I can only find this. No hope of a dry one?' And Martha had run to fetch a dry towel and amazingly found one, and handed it to Katie who flashed her a brilliant smile and said, 'I can't bear damp towels. Anything in the world but damp towels,' as if speaking to a servant in a time of shortage of staff, and took all the water so there was none left for Martha to wash up.

The trouble, of course, was drying anything at all in the cottage. There were no facilities for doing so, and Martin had a horror of clothes lines which might spoil the view. He toiled and moiled all week in the city simply to get a country view at the weekend. Ridiculous to spoil it by draping it with wet towels! But now Martha had bought more towels, so perhaps everyone could be satisfied. She would take nine damp towels back on Sunday evenings in a plastic bag and see to them in London.

On this Saturday morning, straight after breakfast, Katie went out to the car – she and Colin had a new Lamborghini; hard to imagine Katie in anything duller – and came back waving a new Yves St Laurent towel. 'See! I brought my own, darlings.'

They'd brought nothing else. No fruit, no meat, no vegetables, not even bread, certainly not a box of chocolates. They'd gone off to bed with alacrity, the night before, and the spare room rocked and heaved: well, who'd want to do washing-up when you could do that, but what about the children? Would they get confused? First Colin and Janet, now Colin and Katie?

Martha murmured something of her thoughts to Martin,

who looked quite shocked. 'Colin's my best friend. I don't expect him to bring anything,' and Martha felt mean. 'And good heavens, you can't protect the kids from sex for ever; don't be so prudish,' so that Martha felt stupid as well. Mean, complaining, and stupid.

Janet had rung Martha during the week. The house had been sold over her head, and she and the children had been moved into a small flat. Katie was trying to persuade Colin to cut down on her allowance, Janet said.

'It does one no good to be materialistic,' Katie confided. 'I have nothing. No home, no family, no ties, no possessions. Look at me! Only me and a suitcase of clothes.' But Katie seemed highly satisfied with the me, and the clothes were stupendous. Katie drank a great deal and became funny. Everyone laughed, including Martha. Katie had been married twice. Martha marvelled at how someone could arrive in their mid-thirties with nothing at all to their name, neither husband, nor children, nor property and not mind.

Mind you, Martha could see the power of such helplessness. If Colin was all Katie had in the world, how could Colin abandon her? And to what? Where would she go? How would she live? Oh, clever Katie.

'My teacup's dirty,' said Katie, and Martha ran to clean it, apologising, and Martin raised his eyebrows, at Martha, not Katie.

'I wish *you'd* wear scent,' said Martin to Martha, reproachfully. Katie wore lots. Martha never seemed to have time to put any on, though Martin bought her bottle after bottle. Martha leapt out of bed each morning to meet some emergency – miaowing cat, coughing child, faulty alarm clock, postman's knock – when was Martha to put on scent? It annoyed Martin all the same. She ought to do more to charm him.

Colin looked handsome and harrowed and younger than Martin, though they were much the same age. 'Youth's catching,' said Martin in bed that night. 'It's since he found Katie.' Found, like some treasure. Discovered; something exciting and wonderful, in the dreary world of established spouses.

On Saturday morning Jasper trod on a piece of wood ('Martha, why isn't he wearing shoes? It's too bad': Martin) and Martha took him into the hospital to have a nasty splinter removed. She left the cottage at ten and arrived back at one, and they were still sitting in the sun, drinking, empty bottles glinting in the long grass. The grass hadn't been cut. Don't forget the bottles. Broken glass means more mornings at the hospital. Oh, don't fuss. Enjoy yourself. Like other people. Try.

But no potatoes peeled, no breakfast cleared, nothing. Cigarette ends still amongst old toast, bacon rind and marmalade. 'You could have done the potatoes,' Martha burst out. Oh, bad temper! Prime sin. They looked at her in amazement and dislike. Martin too.

'Goodness,' said Katie. 'Are we doing the whole Sunday lunch bit on Saturday? Potatoes? Ages since I've eaten potatoes. Wonderful!'

'The children expect it,' said Martha.

So they did. Saturday and Sunday lunch shone like reassuring beacons in their lives. Saturday lunch: family lunch: fish and chips. ('So much better cooked at home than bought': Martin) Sunday. Usually roast beef, potatoes, peas, apple pie. Oh, of course. Yorkshire pudding. Always a problem with oven temperatures. When the beef's going slowly, the Yorkshire should be going fast. How to achieve that? Like big bosom and little hips.

'Just relax,' said Martin. 'I'll cook dinner, all in good time. Splinters always work their own way out: no need to have taken him to hospital. Let life drift over you, my love. Flow with the waves, that's the way.'

And Martin flashed Martha a distant, spiritual smile. His hand lay on Katie's slim brown arm, with its many gold bands.

'Anyway, you do too much for the children,' said Martin. 'It isn't good for them. Have a drink.'

So Martha perched uneasily on the step and had a glass of cider, and wondered how, if lunch was going to be late, she would get cleared up and the meat out of the marinade for the rather formal dinner that would be expected that evening. The marinaded lamb ought to cook for at least four hours in a low oven; and the cottage oven was very small, and you couldn't use that and the grill at the same time and Martin liked his fish grilled, not fried. Less cholesterol.

She didn't say as much. Domestic details like this were very boring, and any mild complaint was registered by Martin as a scene. And to make a scene was so ungrateful.

This was the life. Well, wasn't it? Smart friends in large cars and country living and drinks before lunch and roses and bird song – 'Don't drink *too* much,' said Martin, and told them about Martha's suspended driving licence.

The children were hungry so Martha opened them a can of beans and sausages and heated that up. ('Martha, do they have to eat that crap? Can't they wait?': Martin)

Katie was hungry: she said so, to keep the children in face. She was lovely with children – most children. She did not particularly like Colin and Janet's children. She said so, and he accepted it. He only saw them once a month now, not once a week.

'Let me make lunch,' Katie said to Martha. 'You do so much, poor thing!'

And she pulled out of the fridge all the things Martha had put away for the next day's picnic lunch party – Camembert cheese and salad and salami and made a wonderful tomato salad in two minutes and opened the white wine – 'not very cold, darling. Shouldn't it be chilling?' – and had it all on the table in five amazing competent minutes. 'That's all we need, darling,' said Martin. 'You are funny with your fish-and-chip Saturdays! What could be nicer than this? Or simpler?'

Nothing, except there was Sunday's buffet lunch for nine gone, in place of Saturday's fish for six, and would the fish stretch? No. Katie had had quite a lot to drink. She pecked Martha on the forehead, 'Funny little Martha,' she said. 'She reminds me of Janet. I really do like Janet.' Colin did not want to be reminded of Janet, and said so. 'Darling, Janet's a fact of life,' said Katie. 'If you'd only think about her more, you might manage to pay her less.' And she yawned and stretched her lean, childless body and smiled at Colin with her inviting, naughty little girl eyes, and Martin watched her in admiration.

Martha got up and left them and took a paint pot and put a coat of white gloss on the bathroom wall. The white surface pleased her. She was good at painting. She produced a smooth, even surface. Her legs throbbed. She feared she might be getting varicose veins.

Outside in the garden the children played badminton. They were bad-tempered, but relieved to be able to look up and see their mother working, as usual: making their lives for ever better and nicer: organising, planning, thinking ahead, side-stepping disaster, making preparations, like a mother hen, fussing and irritating: part of the natural boring scenery of the world.

On Saturday night Katie went to bed early: she rose from her chair and stretched and yawned and poked her head into the kitchen where Martha was washing saucepans. Colin had cleared the table and Katie had folded the napkins into pretty creases, while Martin blew at the fire, to make it bright. 'Good night,' said Katie.

Katie appeared three minutes later, reproachfully holding out her Yves St Laurent towel, sopping wet. 'Oh dear,' cried Martha. 'Jenny must have washed her hair!' And Martha was obliged to rout Jenny out of bed to rebuke her, publicly, if only to demonstrate that she knew what was right and proper. that meant Jenny would sulk all weekend, and that meant a treat or an outing midweek, or else by the following week she'd be having an asthma attack. 'You fuss the children too much,' said Martin. 'That's why Jenny has asthma.' Jenny was pleasant enough to look at, but not stunning. Perhaps she was a disappointment to her father? Martin would never say so, but Martha feared he thought so.

An egg and an orange each child, each day. Then nothing too bad would go wrong. And it hadn't. The asthma was very mild. A calm, tranquil environment, the doctor said. Ah, smile, Martha, smile. Domestic happiness depends on you. 21 x 52 oranges a year. Each one to be purchased, carried, peeled and washed up after. And what about potatoes. 12 x 52 pounds a year? Martin liked his potatoes carefully peeled. He couldn't bear to find little cores of black in the mouthful. ('Well, it isn't very nice, is it?': Martin)

Martha dreamt she was eating coal, by handfuls, and liking it.

Saturday night. Martin made love to Martha three times. Three times? How virile he was, and clearly turned on by the sounds from the spare room. Martin said he loved her. Martin always did. He was a courteous lover; he knew the importance of foreplay. So did Martha. Three times.

Ah, sleep. Jolyon had a nightmare. Jenny was woken by a moth. Martin slept through everything. Martha pottered about the house in the night. There was a moon. She sat at the window and stared out into the summer night for five minutes, and was at peace, and the went back to bed because she ought to be fresh for the morning.

But she wasn't. She slept late. The others went out for a walk. They'd left a note, a considerate note: 'Didn't wake you. You looked tired. Had a cold breakfast so as not to make too much mess. Leave everything 'til we get back.' But it was ten o'clock, and guests were coming at noon, so she cleared away the bread, the butter, the crumbs, the smears, the jam, the spoons, the spilt sugar, the cereal, the milk (sour by now) and the dirty plates, and swept the floors, and tidied up quickly, and grabbed a cup of coffee, and prepared to make a rice and fish dish, and a chocolate mousse and sat down in the middle to eat a lot of bread and jam herself. Broad hips. She remembered the office work in her file and knew she wouldn't be able to do it. Martin anyway thought it was ridiculous for her to bring work back at the weekends. 'It's your holiday,' he'd say. 'Why should they impose?' Martha loved her work. She didn't have to smile at it. She just did it.

Katie came back upset and crying. She sat in the kitchen while Martha worked and drank glass after glass of gin and bitter lemon. Katie liked ice and lemon in gin. Martha paid for all the drink out of her wages. It was part of the deal between her and Martin – the contract by which she went out to work. All things to cheer the spirit, otherwise depressed by a working wife and mother, were to be paid for by Martha. Drink, holidays, petrol, outings, puddings, electricity, heating: it was quite a joke between them. It didn't really make any difference: it was their joint money, after all. Amazing how Martha's wages were creeping up, almost to the level of Martin's. One day they would overtake. Then what?

Work, honestly, was a piece of cake.

Anyway, poor Katie was crying. Colin, she'd discovered, kept a photograph of Janet and the children in his wallet. 'He's not free of her. He pretends he is, but he isn't. She has him by a stranglehold. It's the kids. His bloody kids. Moaning Mary and that little creep Joanna. It's all he thinks about. I'm nobody.'

But Katie didn't believe it. She knew she was somebody all right. Colin came in, in a fury. He took out the photograph and set fire to it, bitterly, with a match. Up in smoke they went. Mary and Joanna and Janet. The ashes fell on the floor. (Martha swept them up when Colin and Katie had gone. It hardly seemed polite to do so when they were still there.) 'Go back to her,' Katie said. 'Go back to her. I don't care. Honestly, I'd rather be on my own. You're a nice old-fashioned thing. Run along then. Do your thing, I'll do mine. Who cares?'
'Christ, Katie, the fuss! She only just happens to be in the photograph. She's not there on purpose to annoy. And I do feel bad about her. She's been having a hard time.'
'And haven't you, Colin? She twists a pretty knife, I can tell you. Don't you have rights too? Not to mention me. Is a little loyalty too much to expect?'

They were reconciled before lunch, up in the spare room. Harry and Beryl Elder arrived at twelve-thirty. Harry didn't like to hurry on Sundays; Beryl was flustered with apologies for their lateness. They'd brought artichokes from their garden. 'Wonderful,' cried Martin. 'Fruits of the earth? Let's have a wonderful soup! Don't fret, Martha. I'll do it.'

'Don't fret.' Martha clearly hadn't been smiling enough. She was in danger, Martin implied, of ruining everyone's weekend. There was an emergency in the garden very shortly – an elm tree which had probably got Dutch elm disease – and Martha finished the artichokes. The lid flew off the blender and there was artichoke purée everywhere. 'Let's have lunch outside,' said Colin. 'Less work for Martha.'

Martin frowned at Martha: he thought the appearance of martyrdom in the face of guests to be an unforgivable offence.

Everyone happily joined in taking the furniture out, but it was Martha's experience that nobody ever helped to bring it in again. Jolyon was stung by a wasp. Jasper sneezed and sneezed from hay fever and couldn't find the tissues and he wouldn't use loo paper. ('Surely you remembered the tissues, darling?': Martin)

Beryl Elder was nice. 'Wonderful to eat out,' she said, fetching the cream for her pudding, while Martha fished a fly from the liquefying Brie ('You shouldn't have bought it so ripe, Martha': Martin) – 'except it's just some other woman has to do it. But at least it isn't *me*.' Beryl worked too, as a secretary, to send the boys to boarding school, where she'd rather they weren't. But her husband was from a rather grand family, and she'd been only a typist when he married her, so her life was a mass of amends, one way or another. Harry had lately opted out of the stockbroking rat race and become an artist, choosing integrity rather than money, but that choice was his alone and couldn't of course be inflicted on the boys.

Katie found the fish and rice dish rather strange, toyed at it with her fork, and talked about Italian restaurants she knew. Martin lay back soaking in the sun: crying, 'Oh, this is the life.' He made coffee, nobly, and the lid flew off the grinder and there were coffee beans all over the kitchen especially in amongst the row of cookery books which Martin gave Martha Christmas by Christmas. At least they didn't have to be brought back every weekend. ('The burglars won't have the sense to steal those': Martin)

Beryl fell asleep and Katie watched her, quizzically. Beryl's mouth was open and she had a lot of fillings, and her ankles were thick and her waist was going, and she didn't look after herself. 'I love women,' sighed Katie. 'They look so wonderful asleep. I wish I could be an earth mother.'

Beryl woke with a start and nagged her husband into going home, which he clearly didn't want to do, so didn't. Beryl thought she had to get back because his mother was coming round later. Nonsense! Then Beryl tried to stop Harry drinking more home-made wine and was laughed at by everyone. He was driving, Beryl couldn't, and he did have a nasty scar on his temple from a previous road accident. Never mind.

'She does come on strong, poor soul,' laughed Katie when they'd finally gone. 'I'm never going to get married,' – and Colin looked at her yearningly because he wanted to marry her more than anything in the world, and Martha cleared the coffee cups.

'Oh don't *do* that,' said Katie, 'do just sit *down*, Martha, you make us all feel bad,' and Martin glared at Martha who sat down and Jenny called out for her and Martha went upstairs and Jenny had started her first period and Martha cried and cried and knew she must stop because this must be a joyous occasion for Jenny or her whole future would be blighted, but for once, Martha couldn't.

Her daughter Jenny: wife, mother, friend.